Last Days of the Morning Calm

Tina Jimin Walton

Marshall Cavendish
Editions

Published by Marshall Cavendish Editions
An imprint of Marshall Cavendish International

A member of the
Times Publishing Group

Other Marshall Cavendish Offices:
Marshall Cavendish Corporation. 99 White Plains Road, Tarrytown NY 10591-9001,
USA • Marshall Cavendish International (Thailand) Co Ltd. 253 Asoke, 12th Flr,
Sukhumvit 21 Road, Klongtoey Nua, Wattana, Bangkok 10110, Thailand • Marshall
Cavendish (Malaysia) Sdn Bhd, Times Subang, Lot 46, Subang Hi-Tech Industrial
Park, Batu Tiga, 40000 Shah Alam, Selangor Darul Ehsan, Malaysia

Marshall Cavendish is a registered trademark of Times Publishing Limited

National Library Board, Singapore Cataloguing-in-Publication Data

Names: Walton, Tina Jimin.
Title: Last days of the morning calm / Tina Jimin Walton.
Description: Singapore : Marshall Cavendish Editions, [2019]
Identifiers: OCN 1088421046 | ISBN 978-981-48-4130-6 (paperback)
Subjects: LCSH: Korea--History--1864-1910--Fiction. | Korea--Kings and rulers--
History--Fiction. | Min Pi, 1851-1895--Fiction.
Classification: DDC 813--dc23

Printed in Singapore

For my family

PROLOGUE

1882

Thirteen Years Ago

The quick susurrus of her skirt penetrated the sleepy midnight air as the lady-in-waiting rushed faster toward the inner sanctum of the palace. Clutching a set of tattered robes and a flickering candle, she flew down the maze-like corridors that led to Queen Min's chambers. Sudden shouts echoed outside the palace walls. It was only a matter of time before the royal guards would be overwhelmed by the mob orchestrated by Taewongun, the queen's bitterest enemy, and also her father-in-law.

For years as regent, Taewongun had ruled the kingdom with a tight fist, keeping Korea a hermit kingdom, closed to all foreign influence. He purged French missionaries, using the martyrs' blood on the kingdom's shores to stave off further intruders.

The ruthless regent ruled through Kojong, his weak son, soft as clay in the hands of his father. To cement his control, Taewongun arranged his son's marriage to the orphaned Min girl, whose clan had little or no influence in court. With a weak son and an unknown daughter-in-law, Taewongun thought he had secured his power.

But he had underestimated the young girl who had plans of her own. Queen Min had her husband's ear, and when King Kojong came of age for the throne, it was she who demanded the regent step down. She amassed enough power by elevating her own clan members and exiled Taewongun from court.

The ex-regent bid his time, determined to access the throne once more. Times were changing, and the kingdom was opening up to foreign pressures under the new reign. Uneasy with change, many Koreans were upset with the court's concessions to modernisation. The old guards complained and Taewongun listened. It was the opportunity he was waiting for and craftily, he fanned the flames of the disgruntled soldiers. Now, waiting like a hungry wolf at the edge of the dark, Taewongun watched the mob finish their job. Soon, it would tear down the gates and storm the palace.

The lady-in-waiting reached the queen's chambers. Without announcing herself, she threw open the paper-screened *hanji* doors.

"Your Majesty! Your Majesty! They are breaking down the main gate – it's a mutiny!"

The queen woke with a start, but remained strangely calm, as though she had been expecting this moment, and changed quickly into the robes her attendant offered.

From the double pavilion, a bell tolled continuously, sounding an intrusion.

Now disguised in peasant clothing, Queen Min and her small entourage made haste toward the servants' gate. Out through the North Gate, they slipped quietly into the dark foothills. There was only one safe place where she could hide. In a small hamlet, just outside the city, she would go to a modest home that belonged to her well-hidden and little-known younger sister.

Part One

CHAPTER 1

Ji-nah couldn't feel her legs, kneeling as she had for what seemed like an eternity. But the numbness of her deadened legs was nothing compared to that of her mind, frozen with disbelief. The red tassel on the corner of the floor cushion poked through now and then as the hem of the lady's billowing skirt rose in tandem with her animated voice.

"Not even the *day* of your birth?" Lady Cho asked again.

Ji-nah nodded, but bit her tongue, forcing herself to keep her gaze low on the tassel; she must keep decorum.

"Ji-nah was born in the year of the dragon, an auspicious year," Tutor Lim offered with a nervous laugh, ingratiating himself to the lady, who seemed too haughty for a visitor of her station. The Cho family was far beneath the Yi name that belonged to her master. Surely her tutor knew this. Ji-nah cast him a sidelong glance that he couldn't have missed, but he ignored her.

"You recall the story of the manor. Years ago, Master Yi took in the poor infant left at his gate," the tutor continued, blinking strangely at Ji-nah.

"Wasn't it also the same year he lost his wife and child? I hardly call that auspicious," the lady huffed.

"But this child brings her own good fortune," he persisted.

"She would have perished from her lowly birth if it were not for fate's mercy. Why, she didn't merely survive, but she's found favor! Look, she's a *yangban's* ward!"

Yangban, the privileged class of noblemen. One was either born into it or in rare instances, men with means were known to take the state examination to test into the title, but never had it been heard of that a girl of ignoble birth be elevated to such status.

Ji-nah had heard it all her life that she was lucky, like a river carp picked to swim amongst the scarlet and golden koi in the royal palace. She was fortunate, but the reminder of her lowly birth still chafed.

"Master Yi hired me to teach her. I can vouchsafe for her deportment. She is diligent with her studies. She reads and writes —"

"Ack! A good wife doesn't need to know her letters. It puffs her up and fills her head with all sorts of nonsense."

Nonsense? Ji-nah bit harder, filling her mouth with a salty tang. She stole a glance at the lady whose downturned mouth reminded her of a dried mackerel. *This* was nonsense — this discussion over her marriage suitability without Master Yi.

"Four pillars," the lady insisted. "The year, month, day, and hour of birth are crucial for divining such unions. My son is eleven —"

"A perfect match! She's sixteen — a dragon sign."

Tutor Lim's sparse whiskers moved comically as he defended Ji-nah's pedigree. Yet, the tight pull of his topknot above his narrow face gave him an austere and hungry look. The tutor seemed small and crumpled in his ill-fitting robe that hung loosely from his skeletal frame — like a child play-acting the importance of his role.

One at birth and thirteen years later — he certainly knew how old she was. What was he getting at? Unable to bite down any harder on her tongue, she corrected, "You're mistaken. I am but fourteen this year. I was born in the year of the horse."

Lady Cho gasped. "Why, Ga-mun is a rooster. A stubborn horse for my Ga-mun? Inauspicious! It would never work."

The lady stood abruptly, ending the fruitless meeting. When her back was turned, the tutor pulled a long thin bamboo switch from his sleeve and waved it admonishingly at Ji-nah. It was a small victory for Ji-nah's pride, but she didn't know then that she had let a valuable opportunity slip through her hands.

CHAPTER 2

The following morning when her tutor neglected to show for lessons, Ji-nah had her desk moved from the study to the open verandah. She welcomed the break after the previous night's debacle with the tutor and Lady Cho.

"The Master will have enough concerns when he returns. He will be pleased if we took care of Lady Cho's request for him," the tutor had said, convincing her that the meeting was mere formality and that she would be helping the master. But the tutor's sudden interest in marrying her off and Lady Cho's criticism of her lowly birth somehow managed to raise a cloud of doubt, disturbing Ji-nah's peace about her station as a *yangban's* ward. She had thought Master Yi would want the responsibility of arranging her marriage, but after last night, all sorts of doubts arose in her mind, as if someone had stirred the sandy bottom of a clear lake.

Master Yi had always treated her with kindness, and she never lacked for anything, except that of kinship, for he would constantly remind her that she was his ward, not daughter. Perhaps the master would be relieved to delegate such intimate matters to the tutor. The more she thought about the whole affair last night, the more distant she felt from her master.

It was ungrateful for her to have such self-pitying thoughts when she considered her fortunate lot. Here she sat in privilege reading poetry on a desk set up on the verandah, where she could hear the bamboo leaves rustle from the grove beyond the manor. Behind her ran a corridor that led to spacious rooms in the main house, and three wide stone steps led down to the open courtyard, the hub joining the servants' and guests' wings and the kitchen. With gardens and ponds dotting the grounds, the Yi property was grand even by *yangban* standards. It was a fortress, with curved tiles on the roof to ward off evil spirits, and an imposing wall encircling the manor to keep away intruders. No passerby could look in, nor could Ji-nah look out.

Yet despite being ensconced in privilege and protection, Ji-nah was rattled. She decided it was her nerves over the master's long absence. It had been almost two seasons since the royal court had sent him on a mission to Peking. The journey itself was fraught with danger – treacherous roads hiding bandits, wolves and leopards – and now there was danger in the kingdom. Even a secluded girl in her station knew that there was unrest with China and Japan fighting on their soil. Master Yi once told her that for centuries, the two countries had been feuding over Korea like two big dogs fighting over a bone.

He should have been back by now.

She reread the same line of poetry a few more times, but could not retain any of it. She closed her eyes, trying to find peace, while her hand found the pendant she kept looped through the inner tie of her high-waisted *chima*. It hung heavy against her chest as if it were made of iron instead of lightweight jade. Still, she closed her eyes, letting the touch of an old keepsake bring her the small comfort of belonging.

"I brought you some cool barley tea." Amah interrupted her meditation.

She opened her eyes and saw that her nursemaid's gaze lingered on her hand clutching the pendant. Ji-nah quickly tucked it away.

"You're never to show that pendant."

"I thought I was alone," said Ji-nah, but her cheeks flushed, knowing she was breaking an old promise she had made with Amah.

"It was payment to the manor for taking you in, not a keepsake. She would have wanted you to forget your past."

Ji-nah knew what Amah meant. Her birth mother had left the pendant with the swaddled babe along with a letter begging the lord of the manor to take the child as his own, to raise as a *yangban's* daughter. The letter had long been lost, but the pear-blossom shaped pendant with a crooked stem, made from cheap quality jade, was all Ji-nah had of her birth mother. It was an audacious request for a wretched woman to make of a *yangban*, but Master Yi was moved with compassion. He didn't need the worthless trinket. Instead, he gave it to Amah, along with the child, whom she would raise from infancy. Amah, who had recently weaned her own son, Han, raised Ji-nah in the servants' wing for most of Ji-nah's happy and oblivious childhood.

It wasn't until she became old enough to learn her letters that Master Yi moved her to the *anbang*, the inner room of the main house. Her younger self knew nothing of the privilege, only the searing pain of being torn away from the only family she knew. She felt banished, crying herself to sleep in her new quarters, away from Amah and Han. Perhaps it was the nightly tears that moved Amah to give Ji-nah the pendant. "Hold it and feel the smooth jade for comfort," she had said. "But only in secret. No one must see this, especially the master. You would only be insulting him. Remember, you're a *yangban* now."

The pendant was Ji-nah's solace, then and now, and while the master was nowhere near the manor, she knew well enough to keep her secret hidden.

No one shall ever see it. She recalled her promise to Amah many years ago, extending her tiny pinky as her solemn pledge. Amah hooked hers tightly around Ji-nah's offering.

"I shall take a walk in the garden then work on calligraphy when I return," Ji-nah said in a slow *yangban* cadence.

Amah nodded, seemingly mollified by Ji-nah's understanding, and set out the brush and parchment as Ji-nah strode out of the verandah.

Later in the afternoon after her stroll, Ji-nah returned to her calligraphy. She practiced her strokes in silence for the song birds and the rustling bamboo were strangely absent – an odd stillness settled like an eerie calm before a storm.

安
心

Peaceful heart, she wrote, wishing it would transform her own. She studied her handiwork, not noticing at first that her sleeve had dipped into the ink stone. A dark bloom spread on her billowy sleeve. When she pulled away, fat drops of ink fell from her brush onto her *chima*, making an even bigger mess.

A sharp breath whistled through teeth, and she looked up. Her tutor's neck craned over her like a vulture waiting over his prey.

"I was feeling agitated, and calligraphy soothes me," she said, not wanting to discuss the night before.

"You had Han move the entire study to the verandah." He took the switch from his sleeve to poke at her inky garment.

"I didn't think you would mind. Besides, I've been thinking about the master, who should have been back by now. The forsythias have already lost their bloom –"

"A student must follow her teacher's instructions," he cut in. He returned tirelessly to this Confucian principle.

"With all the fighting in the kingdom, the master could have been swept up in the uprisings. Shouldn't we make inquiries of our concern to the palace? How can you not be worried about the master?"

"My concern for the master's safety is not in question here. My concern is that you are not learning the proper conduct of a *yangban*." He paused. "You embarrassed me last night – in front of Lady Cho. As a woman, you must be yielding to those above you. Perhaps your coarseness is ingrained in your blood."

A rush of heat prickled her back. She bit her lip, trying to keep her temper in check.

"Do you recall the *eum-yang* principle?"

She nodded. He was getting her back for making him lose face before Lady Cho.

"Then recite it." He crossed his arms behind his back and waited.

"*Eum-yang* is the dualistic principle governing the universe. The moon is *eum* and the sun *yang*; the earth is *eum* and sky *yang*; and woman is *eum* and man *yang*. The perfect balance of *eum-yang* brings harmony into the world."

"Yes, yes that is right. Then you should know inner affairs are also *eum* and outer *yang*. Therefore, a woman should concern herself with only matters that pertain to the home, not the outer affairs of society. You are close to marital age. No one will want a woman who does not know her place."

As the tutor chastised her, the manor gate rumbled open, and she leapt up, thinking it was the master's return. She rushed down the corridor, ignoring her tutor's instructions to walk fittingly for a *yangban*.

In the middle of the courtyard, Amah and Han were receiving a runner who looked on the verge of collapsing. Amah sent Han to fetch water for the sweaty runner that was doubled over and breathing heavily.

A bony hand gripped Ji-nah's shoulder from behind and pulled her against the large wooden pillar. "You'll be seen," Tutor Lim hissed in her ear before making his way to the runner. Ji-nah peered around the pillar, making sure to keep her body hidden from the gaze of a male stranger.

Han returned with a bowl of water, which the young runner gulped in one long breath. After wiping his chin on his sleeve, he opened his pouch and produced two rolled-up scrolls. "I bring message to the Yi Manor." He looked about Han's age, maybe seventeen, for he still wore his hair in a single long braid, rather than a man's topknot. His face was clear and smooth, but for a plum-colored mar that ran along his left temple. Ji-nah did not recognise him as part of the master's entourage.

Amah took the letters from the runner and squinted at the lettering. "Who gave you these?"

"A nobleman asked me to run them to his estate, the Yi Manor in Seoul, before he boarded the ship. He paid me to get them here before sundown."

"I'll handle this," said the tutor, plucking the letters from Amah. Then turning to the runner, the tutor waved dismissively at the boy's hopeful smile. "You said he paid you."

The runner's smile dropped.

"There must be a mistake," Ji-nah said, stepping into view. They all stared in astonishment, except the tutor whose countenance darkened, as if he had bitten into a chili pepper.

"Maybe the letters offer an explanation," the runner said quite brazenly in his reedy voice, meeting Ji-nah's eyes.

Tutor Lim cleared his throat and the runner resumed a servant's stoop.

"Where is the ship heading?" Ji-nah asked, unable to contain herself.

"The *Hinomaru* heads for Japan then to America, I hear," the runner said.

"Master Yi is going to America?"

"He's only the messenger," said the tutor. "Keep him longer and we'll have to feed him." He took the scrolls, stuffed them into his sleeve and headed back to the main house.

Meanwhile, Ji-nah stood stunned, unable to move although everyone was dispersing. Han ushered the runner back to the main gate while she watched the two servants walking side by side – the runner holding his head high next to Han's hunched figure. Once more she wanted to cry out to the runner, the last person to see her master, but she was dumbstruck. Master Yi was not returning.

"Wait! The letters!" she cried, running after the tutor.

CHAPTER 3

Han accepted his lot. A servant serves his master, and fortunately, he had a good master who sometimes let him forget his lowly role and treated him with dignity. But to answer to those who see themselves on equal footing as his master? That was quite another matter. He wasn't thinking about Ji-nah, who had had him move practically everything from the study to the verandah. It was his duty to serve her; she was the master's ward, even if he had grown up with her like his own sister. Years ago when she was moved to the *anbang,* Han had learned that she was to be groomed as *yangban,* and over the years he grew to understand what that meant – a permanent gulf that existed between *yangban* and servant. He had gotten used to that.

But what irked Han was the tutor who, of late, seemed to think himself loftier than the servants just because he knew his letters. It was presumptuous of him to receive Lady Cho, thinking he could pawn Ji-nah off to her imbecile son, Ga-mun.

"What do you know of the master's plans for Ji-nah?" his mother had asked the tutor.

"Lady Cho is so persistent. I'm taking the burden off the master," the tutor had replied. "After I deal with her, she'll never consider Ji-nah for her son."

But it sure didn't sound that way from the courtyard the night before. Han could hear the tutor eagerly trying to make a match of the two, even lying about Ji-nah's age. It was a good thing Ji-nah spoke up when she had; who knows what sort of mess the tutor would have made.

When the tutor finally showed up in the late afternoon and saw that the study was emptied, he stormed up to Han, who was sweeping the courtyard.

"Who asked you to move the study furniture out to the verandah?" he demanded.

Han figured it wasn't for information the tutor asked, because who else would Han answer to in the manor? Han obliged anyway. "You were late, and Ji-nah wanted to read outdoors."

The tutor's tightly pursed lips lost its color, leeching instead to his hollowed cheeks. "I'm her teacher! You take orders from *me*." His face was the shade of eggplant as he stormed off to the verandah.

Han shook his head, unable to understand why the tutor was so livid. As Han was finishing up in the courtyard, someone banged on the manor gate.

A runner stretched his arm against the open gate and struggled for air. "Is this the Yi Manor?" he asked in an accent Han couldn't place. It seemed foreign though the runner wore Korean clothing and a youth's long braid.

Before Han could find out what business the runner had with the manor, his mother swooped in and told Han to fetch the boy a drink. When Han returned, the runner gulped the water greedily.

"A nobleman asked me to run them to his estate, the Yi Manor in Seoul, before he boarded the ship." He handed his mother two scrolls. At this, Ji-nah shocked them all by showing herself before a stranger and demanding, "Where is the ship heading?"

From the corner of his eyes, Han caught the runner brazenly staring straight at Ji-nah, instead of stooping his head, like any commoner might before a *yangban* lady. "The *Hinomaru* heads for Japan then to America," the runner said.

The tutor snatched the scrolls from his mother and dismissed the runner away. The whole scene unfolded like a strange mystery that Han had yet to fully grasp. Upon returning, his mother called out, "Tutor Lim, Ji-nah wants the letters!"

From the shadow of the hallway, the tutor's small figure emerged. He approached the courtyard with a deeper shade of purple resurfacing on his complexion.

"It would be best if I had a look first," the tutor began. "It might be disturbing news."

"If Master Yi sent word, he meant it for me," Ji-nah said.

"Very well," said the tutor, reaching into his sleeve and pulling out two scrolls. A purple cord, caught on the edge of a scroll, dangled from his arm, but the tutor quickly tucked it back into the dark recess of his sleeve. Han noticed Ji-nah staring intently at the cord, but when the tutor waved the letters before her, she quickly unrolled the first scroll. Her eyes swept over the parchment.

"Read it aloud," said his mother.

"I can't believe this," Ji-nah said. "It looks like a will."

The tutor cleared his throat and plucked the scroll that Ji-nah held loosely. He read:

I, Yi Yong-gi, entrust the Yi Estate to Lim Bu Myong from this day forward until the day of my return. All property shall remain his possession if Buddah should not find it favorable for my return.

10 May 504 in the reign of King Kojong

A tight smile formed creases around the corners of the tutor's mouth.

"I don't understand," said Ji-nah.

"I, too, am stunned," said the tutor. "It is a great honor and responsibility I now bear."

Han glanced over at his mother to see if she understood the meaning it all, and saw that under her furrowed brows there was hurt in her eyes. He understood his mother's wounded expression – the responsibility of the manor often fell upon her during the master's many travels. To entrust the manor to the tutor was a sharp sting. Did the master think he may never return?

"Read the other letter," Han urged Ji-nah.

Ji-nah unrolled the next parchment. This time she cleared her throat and began:

Dearest Ji-nah,
I have not kept my promise to return sooner.
China, a great host nation, has given us security
in this past age. I have done
all my duty in China and take the Hinomaru
to America via Japan.
Please, you must not worry.
Instead, you must trust your tutor
and listen to Lim. When I finish my
service to our queen, I promise to
return safely. Be in good spirits and let not
these times of danger keep you from
your studies. Must go.
I will return to the manor, Fate willing and finish my
duty to the court.

Lastly, the classics, like the Annals of the Four Seasons will be a guide to solving all matters.

I write this with my own hand.
Yi Yong-Gi

"Why would the master go to America again?" Han wondered aloud. It wasn't his place to question the letter from the master, but by the look on the faces of Ji-nah and his mother, he knew they were thinking the same.

"I'm equally perplexed," said Ji-nah. "It's a journey that takes months, perhaps a year or more. Why would Queen Min send him on such a treacherous journey without allowing him to come home to tell us in person?"

"King Kojong is still enthroned. Remember, the *court* sent him, not the queen," corrected the tutor. "And who knows? It must be an urgent matter that couldn't wait for the next departing steamer."

Han watched Ji-nah chew the bottom of her lip as she contemplated the tutor's explanation.

"But America, it's such a dangerous place!" his mother burst out.

"I agree with you, Amah," said the tutor. "Westerners are barbarians. They know nothing of Eastern rituals and traditions. The master is a brave man."

"The master is brave for no other reason than to help the kingdom," Ji-nah's voice cracked, as if she were trying hard to be brave herself. "Perhaps the queen sent him to seek help from the Westerners for our kingdom."

"Help? Westerners can't help. They are crude and demanding, washing up on our shores uninvited, imposing their will with cannon fire." The tutor caught his breath, his voice growing shriller. "The east is for the East and the west for the West. *Eum* and *Yang* principle. Don't you remember it? Our kingdom would be better off if Taewongun were back in court."

Taewongun? That old fiend of the court? Master Yi would sooner give the tutor the boot for mentioning the old enemy's name.

"I remind you that Master Yi serves the court, and you wouldn't breathe that foul name if Master Yi were here," said Ji-nah.

"Your master would agree if he could see the state of the kingdom these days. The queen has been far too accommodating to the foreigners. That runner – he was of Japanese descent; did you not know? Our kingdom is becoming awash with foreigners – Japanese and Westerners alike on our soil. For now, it may be only the port cities, but what next? Taewongun would have restored proper order in the kingdom." The tutor took a breath after his small tirade and cleared his throat. "There will be order in the manor, at least. There have been too many indulgences." He turned to Han. "Clear the verandah. Starting tomorrow we will resume lessons in the study. I have much to do today and must prepare to take up residence in the manor. Come!"

CHAPTER 4

Han trailed behind the tutor's vigorous steps to the inn where the teacher had been staying. Even in the shadows of the fading afternoon light, the room was unflattering, with its peeled and cracked oil paper floor and a musty scent of neglect. A sizable chest and an assortment of packed bundles were waiting in the empty room as if the tutor knew he'd be moving out.

"Take the chest, boy."

Han lifted the wooden chest by the fabric tied around its girth. He looped each arms through the ties and wore the heavy chest on his back. The cumbersome load made him falter.

"Careful!" the tutor yelled, then muttered, "Worthless clod."

He was in no mood to argue with the tutor and thought it best to pick up the remaining bundles and head back to the manor before nightfall. "*Jejang,*" cursed Han. As the straps of the heavy load bore into his shoulder, the thought occurred to him that he was now the tutor's servant. With his head stooped, he trudged behind the tutor who hastily picked his way through a narrow passageway along the side of the inn.

A woman came running behind them, yelling, "What's this? Where are you going?"

The tutor ignored her and kept his clip until a gruff-looking man in a dingy white jacket blocked his path.

"Wife asked you a question." The man folded his arms across his chest.

"So uncouth!" the tutor said. "Step aside."

"Insulting me, is it, when you're sneaking off without paying your rent."

"I've settled my accounts with your wife. Ask her."

"You've paid only half month's rent. Said you'd come up with the rest at the end of the month," the woman said.

"Well, it's not even mid-May," retorted the tutor.

"Full payment at the start of each month! You begged me to be patient, and I was. I could have let the room out for double!"

"Double for this place? It's not fit for a dog!"

"*Ee-nom!* Why, you ungrateful cur. Pay up now, or I'll thrash you." The man's eyes promised violence.

There was a standoff in the alley, and Han was sure that if he could see the tutor's face, it would be the same shade of eggplant. But in front of him the innkeeper, with his looming bulk and stray hairs springing loose from his topknot, looked not to be trifled with.

At last, the tutor made the first move with his hand looking to pull out his switch, but instead, he calmly reached around for a pouch tied around his waist. He produced two coins and dropped them before the hulking man. A wild spark returned to the man's eyes, but eventually he bent to pick up the coins. The tutor took this chance to walk past him, and Han followed.

Han wiped the sweat from his forehead with the back of his hand.

When they were a safe distance away, the tutor muttered, "Illiterate beast."

Han turned back and saw the angry man more subdued now and walking calmly with his wife toward the inn. The innkeeper only wanted what was fairly due to him. What did it matter that he didn't know his letters? "You should have settled your account with the innkeeper's wife."

"That stingy woman? I've more than settled my debt in that rat hole they call an inn. I've paid a *won* too many for the watered-down, millet-mixed porridge she calls rice. Humph! The cracked floor makes you boil in the summers, and the crummy paper screen they call a door lets the cold wind blow straight to your bones in the winter. No, that place isn't worth my hard-earned *won*. Good riddance."

"Lucky that now you'll be moving into the manor." Han voiced his suspicion about the tutor who had packed up all his belongings even before knowing he'd be moving that day.

The tutor seemed to be reading Han's mind. "I had it with the landlady. That's why I paid only the half-month's rent. I planned to look elsewhere. Oh, but wonder of wonders! The master has given me a boon!"

Except for Han's labored breathing, they walked in silence. With the heavy load on his back, Han's head was hung low and his eyes fixed on the ground before him. The frayed hem of the tutor's robe flitted with each step. There were threadbare patches and small moth-eaten holes covering the back of the tutor's robe that Han had never noticed before. Though he didn't like the way the tutor treated the innkeepers, Han could understand the tutor's frugality. He didn't have much, it was clear. It was known that the tutor was born a commoner, but he had a patron who found his ardor for classics promising. It was said that this benefactor was supporting Lim's education so that he could take his civil examination. But then something happened to the patron. The rumor at the manor was that Lim, the scholar, took a post as a tutor to pay his debts.

Jejang, thought Han. To rise above your station in life was rough. He had once hoped that he, too, could be more than a servant. It wasn't unheard of. Master Yi allowed him to glean from Ji-nah's lesson and though he did not know his *Han-ja*, the Chinese letters used by the *yangban* class, he was leagues ahead of most servants for he knew some *Hanmeun*, the Korean alphabet used by commoners.

It was early evening by the time they finally reached the manor. Han headed toward the empty guest quarters when the tutor instructed him to clear the master's study and bedroom instead.

"The master's rooms?" asked Han, shocked by the tutor's nerve. "But where will the master sleep when he returns?"

"If he returns, I'll move to the guest quarters. It's the best place for me to conduct affairs."

The master's study was the grandest room in the manor. It was where he received important guests and played a friendly game of *baduk*. "A game of chess with a man reveals much of the way he thinks," the master once told him when Han cleared the chessboard, sorting through the black and white stones.

At the far end of the room, a four-panel folding screen illustrating the majestic Diamond Mountain stood as a backdrop for the entire room. In front of it was a thickly padded mat where the master would sit leaning against a golden backrest, embroidered with a noble white crane in flight. Two large rectangular bolsters supported his arms. There the master would sit behind a desk that had his collection of brushes, ink stone with a dragon engraved mortar, a stack of mulberry parchment, a long bamboo pipe, and a standing oil lamp. The cabinets and shelves displayed his important scrolls and books, ceramics, and even artifacts the master had collected from his foreign travels.

But Han's eyes were drawn to the glass-encased box housing an iron stick, with a smooth wooden handle and a loop for a finger.

"Pull the lever with your finger and it will shoot fire," the master had said, though Han had never seen a demonstration. The master also explained that this was the weapon of the future. "Our neighbor Japan has grown strong in military might with the help of the Westerners' firearms."

The daunting thought of moving the entire study to the storage room made Han sigh. He didn't know where to start and it was getting late. He started collecting the master's fineries, his souvenirs from abroad, when the tutor stopped him.

"What are you doing? Leave the study as is and move my belongings into the bedchamber."

A sliding door connected the study to the master's bedchamber. A wall of cabinets stood like a rank of soldiers from tallest to shortest. Han began to empty the master's personal belongings, his robes, toiletries and linens. But the tutor stopped him once more. "Now what are you doing?"

It was obvious. Since the tutor refused to use the empty cabinets in the guest chambers, Han needed to separate the master's property. Han was collecting the master's silk garments, when the tutor firmly placed his switch on the folded clothes.

"Leave them. There's plenty of space for my paltry belongings."

Han wasn't thinking about space, but more respect for the master's personal property. Yet the image of the tutor's tattered robes came to mind, and somehow Han understood.

Han did everything the tutor asked to prepare the quarters. It had been a long day, and the moon had travelled high in the night sky by the time he could call it a night. He shuffled sleepily across the courtyard to his own quarters, trying to sort through his mixed feelings.

In less than a day, the tutor went from a pauper scholar to an appointed caretaker of the Yi Manor. He still couldn't fully understand his master's choice, but he was at least beginning to. His mother was a servant who could not read; she was as illiterate as the innkeeper. Besides, she was a woman; whoever heard of a woman in charge of an important manor? Something resonated with Han when it came to the tutor who shared his similar background. The tutor's lot offered a small inspiration, and hope stirred. He was determined to learn his letters for it seemed that fortune smiled upon the literate.

Yet, the master's quarters taken up by someone as meager in spirit as the tutor didn't sit well with him, either – however temporary the arrangement may be. But it was seeing the fire stick in the master's study that reminded Han of what troubled him the most. His master was sent away indefinitely to a barbaric and foreign land, and Han was afraid the master may never return.

CHAPTER 5

Ji-nah could hardly fall asleep after the shocking news that the master had revealed in his will. To put Tutor Lim in charge should anything happen was unthinkable, but she had seen the master's script and his seal on the document with her own eyes. To think that he even sent a will meant that there was a chance the master would not return. It was a chilling thought. She read and reread the master's letter to her, and she could not make sense of it. His words meant to comfort her only made her feel uneasy. Even the style of his writing was stilted, even cryptic.

The only person who seemed undisturbed by the runner's news was the tutor, who seemed near elation by his appointment as official caretaker to the manor. He ordered everyone to get him ready to move in immediately. Ji-nah rubbed the smooth petal, trying to calm her mind. But the image of the tutor and his oft-quoted proverbs kept resurfacing.

Where there are no tigers, cats will be self-important.

Master Yi's absence had been known for only a short while, yet the tutor began to order everyone around like a seasoned slave-owner.

A man's heart is exposed when pricked.

Another proverb befitting his outburst on Taewongun. How

the tutor could speak so favorably about the old enemy of the queen and, by extension, her master was a shocking surprise. Did he always harbor such a treasonous sentiment to only reveal it now that the master was leagues away?

If only I were old enough, I would be lady of the Yi house, she thought. The master wouldn't even think of the tutor, if she were of age. She was certain the master, who had no natural heir or relations, was grooming her for the manor. Why else would he consider teaching her politics, philosophy and science, instead of needlework, spinning or fashion? But at the mere age of fourteen and left with illiterate servants, what did she know of running a manor?

If Amah could at least read, the master would have given her charge, as he always did, until his return. She was certain of it. After all, Amah was like family.

Ji-nah tried to respect the master's confidence in the tutor, but if he had heard the tutor's support of Taewongun earlier! Even before the treasonous outburst, the tutor had become irritatingly opinionated, crossing the boundaries of his role. He would sneer when Han joined in on her lessons; just today he had shown up late for lessons, then had the audacity to scold her for moving the desk out onto the verandah. With a long-absent master, the tutor was starting to show signs of authority, and now the master had legitimized it.

Ji-nah rubbed the jade and said a quick prayer to the household spirits – the master's deceased wife, Mistress Yumi, and her unborn child that protected the manor, according to Amah.

"Mistress Yumi and Child Unnamed, bring Master Yi back alive and quickly," she whispered.

With this prayer on her lips, she finally fell asleep well after her oil lamp burned dry.

Ji-nah awoke late the next morning, still half-asleep when Amah set down the breakfast tray with a thud.

"You'd think he's been a master of the manor for years! He's already dictating the menu!"

Ji-nah lifted the stiff linen cover, expecting Cook's usual hearty breakfast: pearl rice, steamed egg custard, broiled fish and kelp soup. Instead, she found a soup bowl of watered down barley porridge and scant condiments of pickled radishes.

"*Aigu*," lamented Amah, "he took the key from me and gave Cook a small ration of rice for the week. What can she make with that?"

The storage room, where the manor's valuable rice was kept, was Amah's domain and she always wore that fish-handled key around her waist like a warden.

"But the master put you in charge of the storage room," Ji-nah said.

"The tutor is changing things around. Said that Master Yi was too indulgent with his servants."

"*Phuh!* He's been in charge of the manor for less than one day and he's criticizing the way the manor is run?" Ji-nah looked at her breakfast tray. "He'll starve us with his stinginess."

Amah sucked through her teeth before sighing, "Oh, America! Why was he sent so far away? Has he done something wrong? The court must be punishing him."

"Don't say such a thing, Amah. Master Yi is respected in court. He would never be banished." While she meant her words, Ji-nah couldn't deny a small seed of doubt taking root in her mind.

After a cheerless breakfast, Ji-nah braced herself for her lesson, which had now been moved back to the study. In the room, the tutor, with eyes half-way opened sat silently meditating, like a stone

Buddha. She shuffled in and bowed to greet her tutor. She felt his eyes follow her as she settled in behind her desk. A book splayed before her meant she was to read it aloud. The tutor cleared his throat and prompted her to begin, but her breakfast rose to her throat and kept her from complying.

The tutor took his switch and placed it firmly on the page before her. "You don't care to read?"

"Forgive me," she said. The morning air was already warm and the room stuffy. With her mind still shaken, she knew it was only a matter of time before she would reveal her contempt. "I cannot seem to concentrate in this room."

"After the debacle the other day, it's appropriate to hold lessons in the study. Do you want Han to move all your things back to the verandah after he's moved them back to their rightful place?"

"No, but I propose a break from lessons today. I'd like to take a stroll in the garden instead. To clear my head."

"It's most discourteous to decline lessons," said the tutor, "though I suppose you would need to clear your head after such big news. But answer me this. Does a river flow upstream?"

She frowned, unsure of his meaning.

"Simple question about the ways of nature. Don't you know?"

"Well, of course it doesn't flow upstream, what does this have to –"

"Because it's against nature. I'm the teacher and it is my role to make proposals. It does not go the other way. That would be against the natural order," he declared with a flick of his switch.

His sudden impertinence left her speechless.

"You recall the poem, *The Three Ways of Obedience*?" He didn't wait for her to respond. "I'm more than your tutor now. I've been officially entrusted with this manor and everything in it. Therefore, the responsibility of the master's ward is by extension mine. The master has been too indulgent with you. You must learn the way of the *yangban*. So again, I ask, do you recall the poem?"

She couldn't decipher his stony expression, yet the edge in his voice cut like the sharp flick of his switch. She had no desire to satisfy her tutor's interrogation, but at the same time, everything he said was true. The master put him in charge and to disobey the tutor was to disobey the master.

She nodded.

"Then write it."

The master put him in charge, was all her mind could hold at the moment. A devilish thought crept over her. She tipped the water pitcher, slowly letting it trickle into the inkwell before she ground the ink stone. Slowly she ground the stone in a leisurely, unhurried manner. She felt the tutor's eyes on her, but she continued to take her time. She dipped the brush into the pool of ink, then tapered the excess on the edge of the well, dabbing the brush gently before repeating the process. Dip, taper, dab. Dip, taper, dab.

The tutor cleared his throat with some vigor.

Her hand took the brush and let it hover, languishing over the parchment until the point of the switch pushed her suspended hand down. The brush splayed, creating an inky blotch. She looked up in protest, but a malicious grin on his face promised a threat that gave her a sudden shiver, as if ice ran down her back. Her resolve snuffed, she commenced again. This time, her brush moved across the parchment on its own will, finishing the poem.

"Recite it," he said.

She stared at the script for what seemed a long time until the switch came down again. She looked up at him defiantly, but the wicked smile appeared again and a chill ran through her once more.

"Recite it," he repeated, cutting the air with a snap of his switch.

She stared at her own script until the words blurred out of focus.

"I said recite it!"

The stifling air in the room descended upon her all of a sudden with the full force of its weight. It was a losing battle. She had to obey the man whom the master had put in charge.

"*The Three Ways of Obedience,*" she began.

Follow the parents in youth;
Follow the husband in marriage;
Follow the children in age.

The tutor's head nodded in agreement like a pendulum keeping time. "Had you made a better impression on Lady Cho, things might have gone well for you. The prospect of marriage into a *yangban* family is no small matter, especially for a girl in your circumstance. I tried my best to spare you from indignity. But as I see it, you need to commit this truth to memory. For submission is the way of the woman."

He still held a grudge against her for making him lose face before Lady Cho, but why did he care so much about her marriage prospects, and what did he mean by her circumstance? It was as if he wanted to shed responsibility of her, even before he knew she would be under his care. Did he despise her that much?

There was little to do than to comply with the tutor and get back on his good graces. She poured more water to grind the ink stone. Apart from the sound of the lazy ticks of the clock and of stone grinding against stone, the room was quiet enough for them to hear a wheezing noise in the corner of the room.

Tutor Lim held up his hand, signaling her to stop. Han had snuck in quietly and was dozing peacefully in the corner of the room. It was like him to fall asleep from all the chores. His day began even before the sun rose and Ji-nah admired his tenacity to sit in on her lessons rather than lazing around to rest. A sharp yelp broke her thoughts, and in an instant, the tutor's switch came crashing down on the sleeping servant. Han startled awake.

"You dare fall asleep during my lesson? Daily you sit here, a servant shirking your real duties, to soak in the knowledge of *yangbans*. Indulgent. This manor needs order!" The tutor raised the switch over his head once more to strike. He struck Han repeatedly, growing more and more feverish with each successive blow.

"*Ai-ya, Ai-ya!*" Han groaned as he backed into the corner of the room. "It hurts!" His raised arms protected his face, but Ji-nah could see his desperation through the folds of his arms. His eyes were pleading with her. *Do something!*

When she saw the malicious tight grin reappear on the tutor's face as he whipped at Han, she froze. A meek whimper came from her throat and the tutor momentarily stopped, but only long enough for him to cast a sidelong glace, warning her to stay quiet. He beat with renewed enthusiasm.

"A slave wanting to learn," he muttered, as his switch whoosed and whipped. "There will be order! I'll never allow this in my manor!"

The commotion brought Amah racing into the room.

"Enough! Enough!" She blocked the blows with her heavy body.

With switch in mid-air, the tutor froze. His heinous expression slowly gave way and his eyes seemed to come into focus. He wiped the band of sweat from his forehead.

"Have you gone mad?" Amah glared at the tutor.

Han quickly unraveled himself from his mother. The tutor fidgeted uncomfortably under Amah's stare.

"That ought to teach you your place," he said to Han. "Next time you'll think twice before you insult me with your disrespect." He straightened his robe and calmly left the room.

"What happened?" Amah asked.

"Han, he –" Ji-nah's words stuck in her throat.

"I fell asleep." Han shot Ji-nah a hurt look, surely meant for her. She felt a sense of shame that she did nothing to help him.

"Since when does he think he can thrash you?" Amah said.

"He's never liked me being in here," said Han. "He only tolerated it because Master Yi allowed it."

Ji-nah was starting to understand what the tutor meant by "indulging" the servants.

"*Hmph*, the hypocrite! He isn't high born. Where does he get the nerve to keep you from learning?" said Amah. Then, noticing the back of Han's neck, she cried, "*Aigu!* You're bleeding!"

Han rubbed the back of his neck; his hand returned sticky red. In a flash, Han got to his feet and fled while Amah trailed behind him, crying, "But he's not the master! How could he do this?"

Amah was right. The tutor was only a caretaker who was entrusted with the master's property, to care for it as the master had; but the tutor seemed to have plans of his own. Curbing "indulgences," like choosing where and what she would learn, seemed to be the new mission. The way he insisted on her writing and reciting the virtue of obedience made her realize he was serious. Ji-nah couldn't fathom how the tutor had become a different person almost overnight. She clutched her pendant and closed her eyes, but the image of the tutor's malicious grin came back and she felt the shiver all over again.

CHAPTER 6

Though his mother called after him, Han ran down the lane through the cool bamboo groves just outside the manor walls. In the middle of the shady grove, he stopped to wipe the sweat from his brow. A pink mix of sweat and blood smeared on his sleeve.

A fresh wave of humiliation came over him, as his mind played out the beating again. It was the tutor's fault for keeping him up all night, unpacking his things, sorting through the master's wares, and getting the room prepared to his taste.

It was bad enough to be beaten, but then to have Ji-nah watch his shame. He didn't know what made him angrier – the fact that she saw him get beaten up or that she didn't say a single word to stop the tutor. She spoke her mind plenty when it suited her – even made herself seen before a complete stranger – yet when it meant risking her own hide, she froze. Gaping at him being beaten, she looked like the crybaby he remembered her to be, following him around wanting to play and ready to burst into tears when he refused.

His back felt hot and sweaty the longer he thought about the whole embarrassing incident. He sent a rock hurling between the bamboo stocks, kicking the stone with his unraveling straw sandals.

He didn't think he resented Ji-nah's good fortune – a common-born girl, treated as a *yangban*. But bitterness and jealously grew in him like weeds he didn't know existed, choking any semblance of peace he thought he had. He wallowed further, wondering why the master didn't adopt him. After all, he was fatherless too, having lost his father the same week the master lost his wife and his infant child. But it was a fanciful dream; even for a generous and unconventional master, such as Master Yi, it was unheard of for a servant to be raised as a *yanban's* son.

He should be grateful for what he had, which was a master who allowed him to learn his letters. It was probably because of his father's tragedy that the master was lenient toward him and allowed him to glean from Ji-nah's lessons. But now, he didn't even have that.

Of all the people, the tutor should understand the master's allowances, but that stingy goat didn't have an iota of compassion for Han. The tutor seemed to want to keep Han from rising above his station in life. He wanted Han illiterate, forever a servant.

Han's feet were unwilling to turn back to the manor. Instead, he walked to the edge of the grove and headed into town, taking a route that took him along a foul-smelling stream. The knife-sharpener, carting his whetstone through the winding lane of thatch-roofed huts and lean-tos, greeted him, but Han stormed by quickly as if a demon were at his heels. He didn't slow his gait until he crossed the footbridge over the stream and reached the broader streets, where the outdoor market bustled with late morning activity. Servants, young and old, carried burdens on their backs; women, some with a child strapped to them, balanced clay pots or baskets on their heads, and beasts pulled wooden carts filled with sacks and vats of goods.

Han headed toward the teahouse, where he frequented from

time to time. The owner, friendly with his mother, knew him and often turned a blind eye toward Han listening to boasts and bawdy stories of her patrons. When she was swamped, she might even put Han to work in exchange for a meal. But today, he wasn't in the mood for jocular banter or even travelers' news. He continued along in his stormy mood, lost in his own woes until spiteful laughter caught him short. It came from a group of ruffians at the edge of the market. Something in the square had their attention, and it wasn't good.

"Look at them – groveling at the white devils for rice."

"It's a disgrace. In the olden days, the public square was for our music, the drums and songs, *pansori* of our people, not some foreign orator!"

"It's that fox, the queen, pandering to the foreigners. But just wait. Taewongun is going to clean this place up, you watch!"

Taewongun again. These men were traditionalists, hating anything modern or foreign.

"East is for the East!"

It was a familiar chant Han had recently heard from the tutor, but coming from this rough group of men, it sounded dangerous. He had a sudden vision of the innkeeper with sparks in his eyes, ready to use his fists.

Han waded through the market, passing stalls with dried fish, soybean cakes and spices. At the square, a mob of peasants had gathered. He saw in the huddle, the object of the angry men's ire: a tall, thin foreigner wearing black, western clothing amidst a sea of peasants in dingy white garments. The man held up a dark book in his hand and spoke in an oddly familiar tongue. Han craned his neck, straining to hear. The white man was speaking Korean!

"… He gives lasting rice. That's the good news!"

The crowd rushed toward him, shoving each other aside. Han was soon pushed into the mix, caught in the wave of onlookers that formed behind him. A stream of men trickled slowly from the mob, tenuously holding a cone of paper filled with grains of rice.

The foreigner was handing out free rice! The mob continued to shove into him, charging like a school of fish, angling for the front of the queue. Eventually, the foreigner shouted, "That's all there is. Save your tracts for another day."

A low groan came from the mob as it quickly disbanded. When the crowd thinned, Han spotted Boram, the Cho family's servant, picking up the littered paper off the ground.

"What are you doing?" Han asked.

His friend looked up squinting, then stared in shock. "What happened to you?"

Han had forgotten how he must have looked. He swiped his arm across his sweaty forehead, which left a rust-colored smear on the back of his hand.

"Oh, this? We have a new master in the manor." Han gave a dry laugh that left Boram looking confused. "Master Yi has been sent to America, and he left a will, putting the tutor officially in charge of the manor until he returns. He was beating a lesson into me."

"What lesson?" Boram looked even more confused.

"Don't fall asleep during a lesson."

"Hah!" Boram laughed, finally catching on. "Lesson? You mean a lullaby." Boram snored and fluttered his eyes, pretending to sleep. "I never understood why you bothered with those boring lessons. If I had free time, I'd take a nice nap in the melon field."

Both boys laughed before Boram returned to his collecting. Boram, who feigned long yawns and made fun of pompous *yangbans*, didn't care about learning his letters. At least that's what he told Han, but Han suspected his friend was saving face. Master Cho, who was typical of most masters, was not one to allow Boram to learn his letters. Master Yi was truly different. He would never call Han an imbecile or cuff him for making a mistake.

Han remembered the time when a salt seller tried to cheat Boram. The sly merchant waved the bill in front of his friend, taking advantage of the boy's illiteracy. Salt was expensive – that's why it had the character for gold as its name – but the amount the salt seller demanded was too much. Yet, Boram would have paid it and gotten home only to get his head boxed by his master. Han helped his friend then, but Han was sure there were many times Boram had been swindled, all because he didn't know how to read. If Boram were allowed, he'd learn his letters, but Han thought his friend was feigning his lack of interest. It was easier to pretend not to care than to hold out for unfulfilled hope.

Han reached down and picked up one of the papers. "What are you going to do with all these?" The foreigner's tracts were folded into vessels for the grains, but when the rice ran out, the people had discarded them all over the ground.

"I wasn't fast enough to get the free rice, but maybe when I bring a stack of free paper, it will please my master. Crumple it up a bit, and it'll be soft for, you know –" Boram made a gesture of wiping his backside.

"What blasphemy!" A voice boomed from behind. The foreigner must have seen Boram's pantomime, for he marched toward the surprised boy and snatched the papers from his shaking hands. "I ought to beat the devil out of you!"

The mention of a beating sent Boram skittering like a stone skipping over water. But the man already had a tight grip around Han's jacket.

"Don't be scared," said the man, who was up so close that Han could smell a nutty scent from him. The man's firm grip tightened, keeping Han's squirmy body from fleeing. Yet however scared Han was, he was captivated by the man's strange features. Flax-colored hair covered not only his head but his pale hands. His nose was as sharp as a mountain-peak and his deep-set, blue eyes magnified behind a set of gold-rimmed spectacles were like marbles.

The strange man seemed equally interested in examining Han. "I'm not going to beat you. You look like you've had your share already. What's your name?"

Han couldn't speak. He dropped his head obsequiously low to avoid looking into the cold blue eyes that looked like they might cast a spell on him.

"The word of God is to be respected," said the man when no answer came from Han. "Looking at your condition, I'd take you in, but you're not a street boy, are you? You must be someone's servant. Go in peace."

The man released Han's jacket, and Han tore out of the market square, as if a hobgoblin was chasing him.

CHAPTER 7

Ji-nah squeezed the blood from her fingertip where the needle made another prick. She had at least a half-dozen wounds as evidenced by the pink streaks on the white sock she worked on. Her fingertips capped with multiple thimbles looked like stubby toadstools. This work was nearly impossible.

"Once you master the basic stitch, then I'll teach you how to embroider."

"Then I shall never learn," Ji-nah sighed.

"I've seen you at your brush strokes. Practice as you would your letters and be patient." Amah took up an armload of soiled linens and left Ji-nah to practice on her own.

It had been a few days since Ji-nah had her formal lessons. After Han's beating, it was never the same. Besides, the tutor had decided that his new duties took on priority and suspended Ji-nah's lessons for an indefinite time. He still thought that Ji-nah was indulged far too much and that she was long overdue in learning more conventional, domestic chores. Ji-nah was more than content with this arrangement for she couldn't imagine returning to the way things were before the tutor's violent outburst.

Though she missed her books, it was a relief to be out of the tutor's way and the servants' wing was a welcome, if dizzying, change of scenery. Amah and Cook created a small whirlwind in their flurry of daily chores. They mulled over meal preparation given their scant budget. They were resourceful though, watering down the cooked barley, or boiling the same oxtail, stretching out its use for the soup broth. They used all that grew in the garden: turnips, peppers and cabbages. They salted everything and preserved them in clay jars kept buried deep into the earth. They cleaned the rooms, mopping the floors on their hands and knees, emptying chamber pots, and gathering mounds of endless laundry.

Ji-nah never considered the amount of labor and sweat that went into preparing her food and clothing, which appeared daily before her like magic. Proper ladies never considered such matters, since they whittled their time on social calls, chatting about the latest gossip and fashion. At least that's what Ji-nah imagined how proper ladies spent their time. Without a lady figure in the manor, she didn't entirely know for certain. But she was positive ladies did not empty chamber pots. Sewing, however, was universal. Even ladies had to learn to sew. And what better teacher than Amah, whose reputation for her fine embroideries was sought after by the most discriminating ladies.

Still, Ji-nah was a slow learner. Fortunately, Amah didn't hover over her, ready to pounce with a switch for a minor offense. Amah's method was quiet, and though she was a servant, she had an air of authority Ji-nah learned to respect from her early years. Even though Amah did not know her letters, she was wise in ways that made Ji-nah think her old nursemaid knew more than she let on.

"It's because he comes from nothing that he has to prove he's something," Amah said about the tutor when Ji-nah complained. "Let him get used to the role and he'll settle down. Each passing day is a day closer to the master's return."

Even as a young child, Ji-nah found comfort in Amah's large, sturdy frame. She remembered those cold wintry nights when old stories of imps and goblins had no power to frighten her because she was sidled up against Amah. But when she was moved to her own room, those sought-after ghost stories only haunted her every night.

Amah would reassure her that there was nothing to fear because good spirits protected the manor. She told Ji-nah to pray to Mistress Yumi and her child for safety because a mother's protection was fierce. Ji-nah imagined the mistress going into the after-life to protect her child. Amah's superstitious advice, in an odd sort of way, made sense and gave her a sense of comfort.

Today, it filled her with courage, as she reasoned that if the master could face the danger of crossing the vast seas to a foreign land, certainly Ji-nah and the rest of the household could endure the despotic tutor. The spirits that protected the manor would ensure it.

A jaunty tune sounded from around the small kitchen courtyard. Han returned with firewood on his back. The whistling stopped when he saw her. They hadn't seen each other since the beating. Han lowered his head, averting her eyes.

"This is my new classroom," she called out a little too loudly, for she was trying to make amends, to make things right between them again. She wanted him to know that the tutor humiliated her as well, keeping her from her rightful place in the inner house.

She held up a limp sock. Han leaned in, squinting at the pink-smudged sock with stitches that ran everywhere except the heel, where the wear needed mending.

"Well, the arch of the foot is well reinforced," he said.

Ji-nah laughed at her own expense, but paid no mind. It was worth seeing his knotted expression give way. The tension was beginning to thaw.

"Tell me what's happening outside these walls," she asked, hoping to draw Han back to his easy natured self.

Han looked unsure, but set his wooden pack down and took a seat on the wooden floor. He scratched his head, deliberating as if he should relay the story, but Ji-nah's eager expression seemed to have convinced him to tell her about the pale foreigner he had been secretly following the past few days. "He's feeding our people, handing out rice. I've been watching him since the day he threatened to beat Boram," he started. Han got more and more excited as he talked on about the foreigner, wondering what kind of people would come so far across the waters to be handing out free rice to natives.

Ji-nah was fascinated and marveled at Han's account, but at the same time, she feared for Master Yi, who would be surrounded by these yellow-haired goblins in America. Her forearms felt like chicken skin and she rubbed them smooth.

Amah returned to find them in idle banter, and though she made a sour mouth at Han's dalliance, it was a feigned annoyance, for her eyes seemed to be smiling at the two on friendly terms again. But the taskmaster Amah couldn't just stand by and hold her tongue.

"A simple errand turns into an outing, Han. I don't know what you're doing these days." Amah slapped her son on the back of his shoulder.

"I'm staying out of his way," Han protested.

"That's what I'm afraid of. What if he wants you and you're not around?"

"I'm his manservant now. I hear his going out and coming in. I'm careful."

Amah had concern in her furrowed brows, but she didn't push it any more. It seemed she didn't want to spoil the rare, peaceful and happy atmosphere.

It had been a long time since Ji-nah had had an untroubled day, and she lay in bed that night recounting all that happened. Then, like hot bubbles slowly rising to the surface, a frightening image of a yellow-haired goblin came to her mind's eye. Thoughts of her master in America scared her more than Amah's old ghost stories. Clutching her pendant, she said a prayer to the mistress and child, the protective spirits of the manor. Then she said one more prayer – to her own birth mother, the one who gave her away – because she remembered what Amah had said earlier in the day: "A mother's protection is fierce."

CHAPTER 8

The last of the apricot blossoms and tender *dureup* shoots gave way to summer's broad emerald leaves. The occasional warm breeze swayed through the branches, making the trees dance in the distant horizon. Shedding his thick cotton jacket, he felt the warmth of the sun on his back and the cool breeze drying the sweat as he chopped firewood for the kitchen.

Early summers reminded him of his boyhood. The long days would allow him hours of play out by the white pines where he was the great Admiral Yi, commander of the *Geobuksun*, the iron ship armada that destroyed the invading Japanese fleet in the Yellow Sea. He smiled, thinking of his younger self, the boy who actually believed he could become an admiral one day.

Gradually, the years taught him the reality of the future that awaited him – years of endless stooping and serving when all he wanted was to lift his head and cast his vision to the horizon. He was bitter about the injustice – the yearning he had, but never the means to attain it. He felt like a starving man placed before a banquet table but forbidden to eat. It was almost better to be ignorant of these tales of great heroes, then he would never know there was such a thing as hunger.

He might still be angry, but for the hope the master gave

him. He hoped that one day he'd have a chance at the state examination that would allow him not only the path of *yangban*, but also the path of military officer. But now his hopes were dashed again. Until the master returned, there was no chance at further learning.

Han picked up the bits of kindling off the ground and brought it to the cook for her kitchen fires. The cook and his mother had been making preparations for the mistress and child's memorial. Every year, the Yi Manor prepared *jesa*, an altar table, to honor the memorial of the dead. The master spared no expense for his beloved wife and child – choice dishes, wine, and incense were offered to honor and comfort the dead. But this year, Han wondered what kind of altar the servants would prepare on such a measly budget.

"Millet and barley are fine for the living, but for the spirits?" Han heard his mother argue with the tutor, but the tutor wouldn't budge. She needed sweet rice for the *songpyeon*, the half-mood rice cakes filled with honey and sesame, which was an auspicious tradition, and a staple at the Yi altar table, but the tutor wouldn't spare anything extra. His mother, however, was not one to be deterred. She told Han to run down to the Cho Manor.

"They owe me a favor for embroidering the bedcovers for their daughter's dowry. A few pounds of sweet rice should be fair. If Master Cho complains, you tell him that Master Yi will see to it when he returns."

It was folly trying to change his mother's mind. She was bent on making these sweet rice cakes, and nothing was going to stop her.

"At a time like this, when we need the favor and protection of the mistress and child, we can't afford to skimp on the spirits."

He went on a fool's errand and braced himself for a clout on the head. Boram opened the back gate of the Cho Manor with one hand and the other rubbing his bright red ear.

"I wanted to repair the master's *ghat*, but the pony hair wasn't strong enough," he explained.

"But you're no craftsman! Mending a *ghat* takes special skill and tools."

"I know that now. I've seen women with their needle and thread. How hard could it be? But I guess I was a little heavy handed and I ruined the master's hat."

Han thought about Ji-nah's needlework and the messy stitches covering everything but the hole. He could only imagine Boram's clumsiness and laughed.

"It's not funny!" Boram protested. "It's because I broke the tip of his pipe that I was trying to save on repairs. He's tough on me whenever I make a mistake."

Master Cho was a demanding master who put such fear in his poor friend that it made things worse for Boram. He would become nervous and make more mistakes, which would cause Master Cho to get angrier. It was an endless cycle of mishap and anger that usually ended with a cuff for Boram.

"What brings you here?" Boram finally asked, dropping his hand from his ear.

"Mother sent me on an errand to borrow some sweet rice. She says the Cho family owes her a favor for the bedcovers … is your master in good mood?"

"Is he ever in a good mood? Are you sure you want to risk it?" Boram turned his head to give Han a good look of his pink ear, but Han feared his mother more than a box to his ear.

Boram led him before Master Cho. Han stooped, looking

down at the tip of his dusty straw shoes and made his request. The spindly man was silent, but Han could feel his critical eye burning the back of his neck.

"For the embroidery?" Master Cho said at last. "That's women's business. It has nothing to do with me."

"It's just a few bags of rice. And when Master Yi returns, he will see that you receive an interest to your loan." It was daring of Han to speak on behalf of Master Yi, but he took a chance, thinking the master couldn't possibly fault him for wanting to prepare a proper *jesa* table.

"You know for certain how your master would repay his debt?"

Han nodded.

"What of the caretaker? Why does he not provide for you?"

Han hesitated in telling him the truth about Tutor Lim's stinginess, in case it reflected poorly on Master Yi's choice.

"It's not for us to consume, but for the altar in honor of the late mistress and child. The tutor is not familiar with the customs of the household."

"Ah, his deceased wife and child. I remember that tragedy," said Master Cho, nodding. "It was well before the tutor, but it is right that he should honor the tradition."

Han bowed deeper, in gratitude for his understanding and for the rice. However, Boram's master wasn't willing to yield so quickly. He continued his interrogation, in hopes Han might slip and reveal manor gossip.

"So, the tutor is the caretaker? Too bad Yi *yangban* hasn't relations in Seoul." He sucked air through a gap in his teeth. "Where did you say he was now?"

Han hadn't said, but he knew word had already spread.

"America."

"America ... interesting," Master Cho said, then hollered, "Boram, you were right for once!" He turned back to Han. "I hadn't heard such a mission in court, but that doesn't mean anything. Yi *yangban's* circles are tighter than mine. I suppose it's all meant to be kept quiet. There's turmoil in the land, and strange things are happening. Court officials are suddenly disappearing from their posts, leaving without a word – hiding, some would say because they're afraid of foreign threats."

Master Cho paused, as if testing Han, trying to tease something out of him. But Han didn't dare look up.

"If you mean Master Yi is not where he says he's going ..." Han said, defending his master, but it was the first he had heard of such a theory and a seed of doubt was cast in Han's mind.

"I never said that. He is a curious recluse, but I'd never question his loyalty," Master Cho replied, as if reading Han's thoughts.

Han cleared his throat.

"Oh yes." Master Cho laughed. "I'll send Boram with the rice later."

"I'll wait for the rice. I wouldn't want to inconvenience you any further."

"No inconvenience."

"If it's the same with you, I'd rather wait."

"You bargain well." Master Cho nodded in mock defeat. "I'll give you your rice, but do me a favor? Next time you go to the market, take Boram with you? Maybe he can learn a thing or two from you."

Han wanted to tell him to teach Boram his letters, so that his servant wouldn't be easily swindled, but Han knew when to hold his tongue. He needed the rice. So he bowed deeply in agreement.

"I take it the tutor knows nothing of your enterprise," said Master Cho.

Han lifted his eyes in confirmation.

The man seemed satisfied and nodded once more before he shouted, "Boram! Get Han some rice."

CHAPTER 9

Ji-nah sat quietly with Amah as the older woman rapidly pushed and pulled her needle with deft skill. Ji-nah made slow progress on her sewing, and even before she had mastered the stitch well enough to learn embroidery, she grew tired of the needle and thread. All the endless work the women did around the house was tiresome to watch and Ji-nah felt she was only in the way, much like a boulder in a farmer's field. The novelty of learning from the servants had worn away and she longed for some peace and quiet with her books and brush, but the tutor maintained that she stay in the servants' quarters to learn the operation of the entire manor, even the lowly affairs.

The tutor seemed harried, attending to the estate. Runners visited almost daily, bringing documents that needed reading and signing. The manor had never seen such paperwork when the master was in charge of the manor, but the tutor explained that with the master's long lapse and his new plans, certain arrangements needed to be made. Meanwhile, he remained frugal and tight-fisted with the manor's spending. Everyone seemed to be making do with the new belt-tightening regime: Cook was becoming creative with her dishes and Amah picked up a few embroidering jobs which she worked on fastidiously.

Now the tutor carried an armload of the master's robes and dropped them in front of Amah.

"I need these taken in," the tutor demanded. "They're too big."

Those were the master's fine robes!

"I will not touch the master's property."

"The robes sit idle. It's a practical thing to do to conserve the manor's resources."

"And when he returns to find his garments shrunken and misshapen? What then?"

"If he returns, he will thank me for it."

If he returns? It's one thing to be caretaker of the manor, but to assume that he is the master by wearing his clothing? The tutor was crossing the line.

"What you ask is inappropriate, and you speak as though the master were not returning!" said Ji-nah, unable to hold her tongue. "Do you wish he never returns so you can pretend you are he?"

The tutor didn't see Ji-nah sitting quietly on the other side, and seemed taken aback by her presence in the room. He cleared his throat. "I'm only doing my utmost for the benefit of this manor, which the master has entrusted to me. As a former tutor, I don't have the finery for my new role, and I don't wish to bring shame upon the manor by wearing unsuitable garments. It is regrettable you feel my request is inappropriate. In these lean times, I will have to spend needlessly on new clothing at the expense of the household." The tutor stepped over the heap of robes in front of Amah, leaving the two bewildered.

It felt like a small victory but without the glory. Why couldn't she hold her tongue? "It is better to rule over your heart than all the kingdom," Master Yi had once taught her. Her careless, angry words only acknowledged her worst fears that maybe the master wasn't returning. How shameful! The tutor was frugal, but also practical, preserving the manor's wealth. What did she know about money and household matters? Perhaps the master was right to place the tutor in charge, so that he would return to plenty. She sheepishly glanced at Amah.

"You did the right thing," said Amah, as if reading her doubts. "I'd rather starve than see that man in the master's clothes. I'll have Han bring the chest when he gets back. Where is that boy? I sent him to the market hours ago."

The mere mention of Han's name seemed to conjure him back from his errand.

"Your burning ears brought you rushing home?" teased Amah. "You still have the good sense to fear your mother."

Han returned the jest. "Actually, it was someone more frightening than you!"

"Did you go back to Master Cho?" Amah asked.

"No, I didn't. I was able to find more rice somewhere else." Han pulled out a large lump from his knapsack.

"Are we so desperately poor that we have to beg our neighbors for rice?" Ji-nah asked. "What has become of our household?"

"It's not for us," Amah said. "It's for the spirits. The tutor is tight-fisted and won't spare a grain of sweet rice for the altar table."

"If he can afford new clothing, why can't he afford sweet rice?"

"He thinks it's indulgent in a time of turmoil. He says he's being prudent with the master's resources," Han said.

Ji-nah had heard all this before, but she wondered why they were in such dire poverty. If the palace sent the master on the mission to America, there was no reason why they would not support his household during his absence. Perhaps the tutor didn't know just how important the master was at court …

"Where did you get that rice?" Amah asked Han, interrupting Ji-nah's thoughts.

"At the market, and it didn't cost a single *won*." Han took the grains from a cone-shaped paper and spilled it into an empty woven basket.

"*Aigu!* Get that away!" Amah waved her hand as if to ward off a curse. Amah couldn't read the *Hangeul* lettering on the print paper, but by the prominent cross, it was clear what had frightened her.

"Is that a foreign tract?" asked Ji-nah, curious to see, after hearing Han's stories about the foreigner.

Han nodded, flattening out the curled edges.

"Han, *aigu*! Are you trying to make the guardian spirits jealous when we need their protection?"

"It's just a piece of paper, and the foreigner was giving away free rice. You don't know how lucky I am to get free rice!"

"No, no, no. This is a bad omen. The foreigner's sign can only bring trouble."

"Are you against the foreigners, too, like the tutor?" Ji-nah asked.

Amah's lip tightened as if she didn't appreciate Ji-nah's comparison, but she nodded.

"Lim's right about one thing. The Westerners are violent barbarians. Up in Pyongyang, a missionary destroyed *jesa* altars, saying they were wicked idols. Do you know what else? One of those barbarians caught a hungry boy taking some fallen apples from an orchard. He yanked the boy by the ear, nearly ripping it off, and branded him – '*todok*' – clear across the boy's forehead with a caustic solution that no amount of soap and water can take off."

Ji-nah shuddered at the thought of having the word "thief" forever stamped on her forehead.

"They're brutal, with no regard for our people," Amah continued. "I heard another story about a foreign devil who pointed a black box at a farmer to take his image. The farmer waved him away, afraid the box would take away his *shin,* but the white man ignored him and took his image anyway."

"Did it?" Han asked.

"Did it what?"

"Take away his spirit?"

"Of course!"

"I've heard of those boxes," said Ji-nah. "Master Yi told me about them. He has an image of a bridge in America."

"Yes, but that's an object. When that thing takes an image of a person, a part of his spirit is etched into that picture, trapped forever. That's why you won't see the mistress's or the child's image anywhere. Their spirits are intact and powerful to protect.

"Let me finish my story. The farmer threw a stone in protest, then do you know what the white man's friend did? He took out an iron stick and shot fire at the farmer's leg! These are violent and barbaric people. Criminals and outcasts from their homeland. Best not deal with them, free rice or not."

Ji-nah never considered the possibility that the foreigners might be exiles, banished from their motherland because they were the worst of their lot. The thought of criminals roaming the kingdom gave her a fresh chill.

But what of Master Yi? Was he exiled? Was he driven away by his country to a barbaric land? She must put aside such dreadful thoughts. Master Yi had a mission.

She noticed Han rolling up the tract, sneaking it back into his sleeve while Amah ranted. "The only way to overcome fear is to learn," Master Yi had once said to her.

She must ask Han for the tract.

CHAPTER 10

His mother told him to get rid of the paper with the offensive cross, but Han wasn't willing to give in to her fears and superstition. Not just yet.

Her tales were terrifying, but he knew her knack for storytelling – and embellishment. She had never seen a real foreigner like he had. Besides, they couldn't all be criminals. Hadn't the man been giving away free rice to his people? Someone so generous couldn't be a pure barbarian. Yet, if the foreigner threatened to beat the devil out of Boram, what's to stop him from burning a word like "insolent" onto Han's forehead?

The tract hidden in his sleeve felt hot, wanting to be read, but it was growing dark and the rest of his chores needed tending. It would be impossible to read it in the shared room with his mother. It would have to wait until the next day.

The tract was written in *Hangeul*, the script for the common folk, not *Hanja*, the characters for the *yangban*. He looked forward to testing his reading skills. While collecting kindling for the evening fires, he made a quick visit to the white pines. In the little niche at the base of the big boulder, Han slipped the paper between the rock and earth.

CHAPTER 11

There was a lone tune coming from the courtyard. A goblin with stringy yellow hair spun around, holding a small bundle in its arms. A warbling sound came from its throat, and it occurred to Ji-nah that the yellow-haired goblin was singing a lullaby to a swaddled baby in its arms. The fair creature seemed to sense Ji-nah watching it and stopped abruptly. Its eyes, the color of pale blue sky stared back at Ji-nah.

She woke with a start. All the talk of foreigners had her mind reeling. But those eyes, the pale, sky-blue eyes on the goblin were troubling. She lay in bed trying to conjure up the old memory she had locked away in a forbidden part of her heart for she knew it was an unlucky thought. Amah had told her to forget and never speak of the incident, because it would only bring bad luck. But if Ji-nah thought hard enough, she could dust away the cobwebs of that neglected part of her memory of "ghost eyes".

Amah said that Ji-nah had an intuition, a sixth sense of some sort because a decade ago, little Ji-nah had helped save Han. Amah didn't have to tell this story, because Ji-nah remembered the incident all on her own. Ji-nah recalled her younger self being strapped behind Amah's back while her nursemaid went about her chores preparing the manor for the master's important guests.

Young Han, too small to help, was sent with a rice ball and told to play in the gardens. Later in the day, however, Amah couldn't find her boy. Ji-nah could still feel the jostling of her panic-stricken nursemaid as she rushed to the white pines, crying out for her boy.

The next part of her memory seemed almost fantastical to be true, yet it was etched in her mind's eye. The most unusual-looking lady with long, loose, ink-black hair stood by the boulder where Han often played. Her white garment seemed to shimmer with brightness and her skin was fair and translucent. She looked like nothing from this earth for she had an odd sort of beauty with arresting sky-blue eyes, unnatural for a Korean. Ji-nah thought she must be an angel, but the woman spoke to little Ji-nah with familiarity, as if she knew her. The woman told her that Han was in the old well.

Amah, who did not see anyone, had to be told by little Ji-nah to check the well. Sure enough, Han had fallen in and was clinging desperately to a large water-drawing gourd.

Amah seemed afraid of little Ji-nah's story, as if the apparition would bring calamity to the manor; but Ji-nah remembered differently. Ji-nah asked if it might be an angel or even the mistress of the manor, only to be told by Amah that those ghost eyes were unnatural and speaking of them would only bring bad luck.

Her dream of the yellow-haired goblin brought back the memory of the apparition with the ghost eyes. She shook the thought away.

She clutched her pendant for comfort and tried to close her eyes once more when she heard something shuffle outside her door. Her eyes widened at the thought of mice, but the sound had more heft than mere mice. She strained her ears, and this time she heard a creak.

All hope for sleep fled. She kicked off the warm, sleep-laden quilt and pulled on her robe. It wasn't rational, but she had hoped it was the master returning, telling them that it was all a mistake and that he was back for good. She quietly slipped out into the corridor. The entire household was dark and asleep, but the moon, high in the night sky, spilled its light at the edge of the dark corridor. When she neared the courtyard, she froze, suddenly afraid of what she might find. She remained hidden, safe behind the pillar. Slowly, she peered around to find the source of the nighttime shuffle: a man dressed head-to-toe in black carrying a sack of rice on his back. They were being robbed!

Amah was right – the goblin in her dream and the ghost eyes were an omen that brought bad luck.

She needed to alert someone, but the servants' wing required her to cross the courtyard, and she was afraid. What if she crossed paths with the burglar? She walked back to the *anbang* to another set of corridors that led to the tutor's chambers.

"Tutor Lim," she whispered outside his door. "Tutor Lim!"

No response. She slid the door to his sleeping chamber. When her eyes adjusted to the dark cavernous room, she saw that his room was empty and his bed undisturbed.

Where was the caretaker? They were being robbed under their noses, and he was absent. She closed the door and ventured back toward the courtyard. She had to do something, if nothing more than to get a good look at the prowler to help identify him in the safety of daylight. She peeked around the pillar again, looking for the dark figure, but there was no more activity. It couldn't have been her imagination for the gate was left open like a gaping jaw exposing the dark belly of the night beyond the manor walls. Had the prowler gone for good while she searched for help?

She tilted her head back against the pillar and closed her eyes, mustering up the courage to close the gate. Gripped with indecision, she wondered what would happen if the burglar returned and caught her. She wiped her sweaty palms along her robe when the hinge of the old gate creaked like aged joints.

To her surprise, a slight figure in a familiar sleeping robe closed the wooden lock and strode across the courtyard toward the storage room.

It was the caretaker, the tutor, who had just helped rob the manor.

CHAPTER 12

Early the next morning, after he tended the morning fires, there was pounding at the gate. A runner came with a letter for the tutor. Han was afraid to wake the tutor at such an early hour, but the runner wouldn't leave without a reply.

"What is it?" The tutor sat up abruptly from his bed.

"A letter came for you," said Han. "And request for a reply."

"Well, don't just stand there. Bring it here and strike a lamp." The tutor, now wide-awake, tore open the seal. His eyes roved over the words and gleamed in delight. Grabbing the lamp off his bedside table, he slipped behind the connecting doors into the study.

Through the open sliver, Han watched the tutor unlock a writing box. Han edged closer to the door where he could see the tutor feverishly searching for something. The lid blocked his view from the object the tutor now seemed to have found. The tutor scribbled something, then looked as if he were stamping the letter with a seal. It was indeed a seal, for now Han could see him wrapping a purple cord around it and placing the wrapped seal back into the box.

Han edged back into the sleeping chamber, away from the door's opening.

"Give this to the runner." The tutor handed him a letter when he returned to the room. "I haven't time to dress."

"He brings good news then?"

"Of course, I've done nothing but good since taking over this estate." The tutor rubbed his hands. "If all goes well, we will have pearl rice! Prepare my washing bowl when you return. I'm getting new robes today!"

The tutor was in a jolly state preparing for his outing, but whatever was the cause for his good mood, he didn't share with anyone else. Instead, he gave Han a long list of instructions for the day, in preparation for his new purchases.

"Take away all of the master's old garments."

"Where shall I store them?"

"What do I care?" the tutor replied breezily, then, after a second thought, ordered him to box everything up and store them. He took the fish lock key from the tie of his pouch and handed it to Han.

Han sighed. Reading the tract would have to wait.

By late morning, Han had helped the tutor get dressed, served his breakfast and ate his own. After the tutor left the manor, Han began his assignment. He hadn't been to the storage room since the tutor took the key from his mother over two months ago. Under his mother's care, the storage room had always been swept and kept tidy. Now, the furniture was covered in a thin layer of dust and the unused threshing baskets were covered in cobwebs.

Oddly enough, though, beneath the hanging baskets was an empty circle where the floor was strangely clean and dustless. The manor's sacks of rice that were normally kept there were gone. They had had an ample supply of rice – at least that's what Han recalled two months earlier – enough rice to provide for the estate well beyond next year's harvest.

Han looked around the room. The sacks were indeed gone.

The tutor was the only one with the key. Up until then, Han hadn't given much thought to what the tutor was doing for the manor. He believed that the man's frugality was in some way a virtue, but the missing rice now raised doubts. Rice was currency. When and how could the tutor have sold it? No one came in the day to pick up the sacks, yet the dustless space suggested it was a recent removal.

Nothing made sense: the letter this morning, the spring in the tutor's steps, and now the missing rice.

He went back to the master's quarters to retrieve the last of the clothing when something caught Han's eye. Through the study's sliding door, a shiny brass key sat perched on the tutor's letter chest. In haste, the tutor must have forgotten to tie his key back to his pouch.

The key beckoned. Han's intentions were downright treacherous, perhaps even ignoble. It was certainly unfitting for a *yangban* to slink through someone's property, but *jejang,* he wasn't a *yangban*!

He flung open the door and took the key off the desk before he could change his mind. Images of the empty space in the storage room and the tutor in high spirits flashed in his mind while his hands remained surprisingly steady, working the key into the lock.

When the lid opened, a thick marble seal with a purple cord wrapped around it rested on a bed of papers. When Han picked up the seal, the cord easily uncoiled around the polished stone. He examined the seal carefully. The *Hanja* character carved backward was difficult to read, but the engraving still glistened with fresh ink. He pressed it into the back of his hand.

Immediately, he recognized the character: Yi.

What was the tutor doing with the master's seal? Even as caretaker, it was not usual to have the master's personal seal.

Han rummaged through the pile of letters written in classic script. He cursed himself for not knowing the *Hanja* letters, but he at least knew his numbers. And there were lots of numbers on those papers. Han could only think of one thing these numbers meant – money. Did the estate owe money? How was this possible when they had been conserving so much?

If only he could read!

He deliberated whether or not to take the letters. It wasn't just that he feared the iron rod for stealing, it was more about his wounded pride in having to ask Ji-nah for help in reading the letters. *Jejang.* He stashed a few letters up his sleeve, then carefully wrapped the purple cord around the seal and let it rest back on its bed of papers.

CHAPTER 13

Ji-nah's breakfast sat cold in the corner of the room; she had overslept again. Last night's robbery seemed like a bad dream, but the nightmare was real, as her discarded robe laying inside out would attest.

If the tutor hadn't stirred about until the predawn hours, she might have awoken Amah and Han the previous night to tell them about the robbery. But in the late hours, she wasn't ready to confront the tutor about his strange activity, helping the mysterious man in all black. She needed time to think.

All night she wrestled with speculations and this morning she was still left baffled. Why was the tutor helping a robbery? She dressed quickly, changing the pendant from her sleeping gown to a fresh *chima*. The jade felt heavy and insistent, as if it too were expecting something unfavorable. It was an absurd idea, but Ji-nah believed her pendant had a personality, almost as if it knew when an ill portent lurked close by.

In the small courtyard outside the kitchen, Cook was alone, feverishly pounding the sweet rice to make rice cakes.

"Where is Amah?" Ji-nah asked.

"Out," said Cook. "But Han's around – somewhere."

"What about the tutor?"

The cook grunted something about new clothes. Ji-nah went looking for Han, thanking the spirits that the tutor was away. She crossed the main courtyard and came upon the opened storage room. She wondered if it was left open after last night, but she distinctly remembered the tutor shutting and locking the storage room. Was this a coincidence?

She stepped into the cool, dark room, the scene of last night's burglary. Even in the light of day, the room had an uninviting feel. The hulking shapes beneath the burlap were only furniture, but in the dimly lit room, they looked like specters. Old chests, cabinets and vats lined the side walls, and opposite the entrance a row of dusty threshing baskets clung against the wall. Ji-nah made her way through the aisle of boxes and chests to where a small light shone from the middle of the room. She found Han in midst of piles of garments.

"What's wrong?" he asked.

She couldn't hide the worry on her face, and blurted out, "I think we were robbed last night!"

Han's eye grew wide. "What are you saying?"

"Where is the rice kept?" she asked.

Han jerked his head toward the back wall and pointed to the empty space. "There were stacks beneath those baskets … but I noticed this morning that all the rice is gone! How –"

"Last night, I saw the robbery!" She carefully explained all she had seen the night before: the prowler in black carrying sacks of rice through their front gate, aided by Tutor Lim.

Han slowly began to nod as if pieces of a puzzle in his mind were starting to fit together. "I noticed this morning the missing rice. I knew the tutor had to be involved – he's the only one with the key to the storage."

"But why would he steal from us?"

"Because he's greedy and he's taking the spoils before the master returns? I don't know, but you say the prowler was covered in all black, even his face? I've heard talk at the teahouse stories of Japanese mercenaries in the kingdom. Supposedly they wear all black and move like shadows. I wonder if the thief was Japanese."

"But why would Tutor Lim help a Japanese? He hates foreigners – all foreigners," said Ji-nah.

Han looked as if he were in deep thought, mulling over something in his mind before he finally said, "I have something to share with you. I think this is important and may answer some of our questions." He pulled out a parchment from his sleeve. The broken seal formed two halves of a geometric pattern that belonged to the royal court. Ji-nah scanned the letter, bewildered by the implication. Only after several more reads did the mystery of her master's situation start to sink in.

"What does it say?" Han asked.

She shook her head in disbelief. "Where did you get this?"

"I took it from the tutor's letter chest. I'm not proud of how I got it, but I have my reasons."

Ji-nah didn't care that Han took it from the tutor, she only wanted to make sure it was authentic. "It's a royal fine, charging the master for failing to appear before a summons. I don't understand why the master is going to America if the court did not send him. What could be the meaning behind this?"

"Is it possible the tutor had been paying the fee with the rice? Maybe that's why he has been so frugal. Master Cho mentioned that there's so much uncertainty in court that some officials were abandoning their duties. Master Yi could – "

Ji-nah's cold stare stopped him short. "That's not possible," she said, shaking her head. "He would never abandon his duties in court, nor his obligation to his manor. He's no coward." While she meant every word she said, she couldn't deny the evidence before her. Han's logic seemed to make the most sense, but still in her heart she refused to believe that the master got scared for his life and tried to save his own skin by leaving for America. That seemed almost impossible, but why would he be leaving on a ship if the court did not send him? Where was he going?

"I'm not calling him a coward," said Han. "It's just that nothing else seems to explain – "

"He's no coward!" Ji-nah shouted.

Han's eyes grew wide with fear, and Ji-nah felt vindicated, as if she finally settled the wretched thought in Han's mind, but Han's frozen expression was fixed on something behind her. The hairs on the back of her neck stood up and a chill ran through her body.

"What is the meaning of this?" asked the tutor, snatching the letter from her hand.

Blood rushed to her head, drowning out all sound but her own racing heartbeat. How much had he heard? She hoped Han's face would reveal some answers, but he was stooped now, his face replaced by the crown of his head.

"Where did you get this?" he demanded.

Han mumbled incoherently.

"Stealing my property?" he said to Han. "As if to find you fraternizing with a lady isn't bad enough! I have the right to sell you, you snooping vile thief!" He yanked Han by the braid, muttering curses while leading him toward the door.

"Thief? I should ask you. Where is the manor's rice?" Ji-nah's voice cracked but her tone was calm.

The tutor froze in his tracks.

"I saw you," she continued. "Last night. I saw you helping a man in black take rice from the storage room."

The tutor had his back toward her. He remained still for a long while as if he were bracing himself for something. If only she could see his face, she might be able to discern the truth. But all she sensed from his back was his anger leaching like poison.

"You think I'm stealing from this manor," said the tutor finally, slowly turning around. "You think I'm keeping the spoils, getting fat and rich while I deprive you of your comforts?"

She stayed silent, knowing better than to play into his trap.

"You think I go buying fancy robes while you all suffer?" he said, sounding wounded. "Well, this letter Han stole from me should tell you that your precious master is not as noble as you think. He shirked his duty to the court and now we are paying for his dishonor. This fine is only the beginning. There's a fine for fleeing, and I'm paying the court for his cowardice."

Ji-nah refused to believe the tutor's explanation. The master wouldn't desert them – his country, his manor, his ward. "That can't be so. He's going to America on a mission. He said so in his letter. It must be a covert mission that only a few in the inner circle know of – "

"All a ruse," the tutor said. "We were all duped. He's a deserter. I'm trying to salvage the reputation of the manor, but you two are sneaking around and stealing letters from my – "

"That is a lie," Ji-nah cut him off. She couldn't bear his accusations, and something about the tutor's story didn't make sense. "The man in black last night – he was no court official. Who pays debts in the middle of the night?"

The tutor's lips tightened, disappearing into a menacing gash.

"Who was he?" she demanded.

The tutor growled, muttering curses. "You interrogate *me*? I owe no one an explanation. You're at fault here, sneaking around the manor and scheming with this thief. And you!" He resumed his grip on Han's braid and dragged him out of the storeroom. "I'll see you sold before the day is through!"

Ji-nah ran after them. The ruckus brought Amah out into the courtyard where Han was kneeling in the dirt.

"They were fraternizing in the storeroom, sullying the reputation of my manor. Were you aware of it, woman?" the tutor boomed. "Furthermore, your son stole from me. I won't stand for theft. Someone must be punished, and I say he will be sold today."

Amah's eyes widened in terror when she realized the severity of the tutor's threat. "No, please! He will never do it again!" She turned to Han. "Whatever you did, apologize to the tutor."

Han bowed his forehead touching the ground as he begged for forgiveness. But the tutor was not appeased. Ji-nah had made him lose face, and he would take it out on Han.

"Please don't sell Han," Amah begged, prostrating herself at the tutor's feet.

"This cannot go unpunished," he said. "I've already thrashed him once before. He hasn't learned. He must be gone today."

"Please," sobbed Amah. "The master would never do something like this. He'd never break up a family."

"He's a fool then, to keep an idle thief as a servant."

Ji-nah couldn't stand by anymore. "I'm the one who approached Han," she said above Amah's wailing and pleading. "If anyone is to be punished, it shall be me." She trembled, but never felt braver.

The courtyard grew silent as the tutor combed his fingers through his beard, contemplating her proposal.

"Very well," he said at last. "Have it your way. Twenty lashes."

The tutor ordered Amah to carry out the beating since it wouldn't be appropriate for him to see Ji-nah's bare skin. It wasn't a real choice for Amah, whose refusal meant seeing her son sold off to another household. Ji-nah took Amah's hand and gave it a gentle squeeze.

Before the day was through, Ji-nah stood on top of a teetering stool holding up her skirt and exposing her white calves. Amah held a thick rod, ready to mete out the punishment. Ji-nah took comfort knowing that she could do something for the manor by saving Han this time.

It will soon be over, she thought.

"The lashing must fit the punishment," the tutor ordered from the hallway behind the closed door. "Go too soft, and I'll have you do forty!"

CHAPTER 14

If it weren't for his mother's wailing, Han would have gladly suffered the punishment than watch her beg like a pitiful dog. Being sold would have been nothing. If the master could desert the court, surely there was nothing binding Han to the manor.

His forehead repeatedly touched the dirt. But once he heard Ji-nah announce she would take his punishment, he stopped mid-kowtow to sneak a peek. With her proud chin lifted and eyes unflinching, she looked defiant, defending Han, or the master's reputation – possibly both.

Han didn't know what to think. All the evidence pointed toward the master's dishonor, and perhaps the tutor *was* doing all he could to save the manor from disgrace. Strange things were happening in the real world outside. He had witnessed them himself, hadn't he? Angry countrymen flared up against the royal family, friendly with pale-skinned foreigners. What could Ji-nah know about what was happening in their kingdom? Kept inside the walls of the manor, insulated from the stirrings outside, she could afford to keep faith in the master. But not Han. If anything, his one experience with the foreign man had taught him that foreigners were different and dangerous.

Master Yi could have easily fled. Maybe the ship heading to

America was a ruse, as the tutor said, and he had escaped to Japan. But one nagging thought grated on him like a fishbone caught in the back of his throat. He just couldn't make sense of the master's seal in the tutor's possession. Why would the master give away his personal seal? Drafting a will was one thing, but to give away his seal was like giving away his own fingerprint. He wished he had told Ji-nah about the seal, but he didn't have time. Now it was too late. She had declared herself a martyr, and by the sinister look on Lim's face, the tutor seemed appeased.

What happened next occurred in such a flash that by the time he dusted himself off the ground, he was left alone in the courtyard. The argument over the rice, the prowler, and the master's abandonment all faded to the background and the only sound that rang with clear resonance was Ji-nah's last words: *If anyone is to be punished, it shall be me.*

Without looking back, Han ran past the spare room where the punishment was taking place and went to the familiar white pines. There he stopped at his boulder. With his sleeve, he wiped his eyes.

What had he to cry about? Yet, the thought of his mother wailing, begging the tutor and Ji-nah offering to take his punishment brought a mix of shame, sorrow, and anger. The sting of injustice pricked him again, reminding him that he was but a helpless servant. Did he really have no choice?

He saw the wadded-up paper in the notch of the boulder. Was it possible that such a thing could have brought calamity to the house? Maybe his mother was right – the house spirits removed their protection because he had brought in a foreign god. He took the paper, intending to burn it, but curiosity held him. He unfolded it and sounded out the *Hangeul.*

He didn't understand everything he read, but understood

enough that the foreign God was the only one that could save them. He crumpled the paper. No doubt the house spirits would be piqued to jealousy. He walked back toward the kitchen and threw the offending tract into the kitchen fire. He wouldn't allow another calamity to befall the manor.

But the damage was done, it seemed. There was whimpering as he approached the hallway of the *anbang*. His mother, a crumpled heap on the ground, was crying. Awkwardly, he bent down to lift her up.

"Oh, what have I done?" she said.

It was his fault. Had he destroyed the foreign tract when she asked, this wouldn't have happened.

"Is she all right?"

"Brave girl," his mother said. "She passed out from the pain. Cook is helping her right now. I can't bear to see the wounds I've inflicted. Oh, he's a cruel monster. He's turning us against each other. What will the master say when he hears I've whipped his ward? What choice had I when he threatened to sell you? What did you do to warrant Lim's wrath?"

"Nothing but uncover some oddity," Han began to explain. "All the rice – gone. The tutor said he was paying a debt for the master's cowardice. But then Ji-nah saw him last night helping a man in black take our rice. The tutor got really angry. That's when he accused us of fraternizing and said he would punish me for not knowing my place. Then the tutor said the master had done an ignoble thing – a summons from the court shows the master lied in his letters. I don't know what to think." All his jumbled thoughts spilled out of him and he felt a little relief being able to tell his mother.

"Where did you find the letter?" his mother asked.

His face burned while his silence was his own admission of guilt.

His mother seemed to understand what Han had done and the reason for the tutor's wrath. She looked sad and disappointed, but it wasn't for stealing as Han had thought.

"We all have our reasons for being suspicious of the tutor," his mother said calmly. "The master elevating him is rather odd, but why would you believe the court over your master's own words? You think you know everything, just because you know your letters some. Trust what you know of the master."

His mother's wise words put him on solid ground and for a moment he felt his foggy thoughts lift. He wasn't muddled, after all.

The master's seal was a clue that something wasn't right.

CHAPTER 15

Ji-nah raged with fever, going in and out of consciousness with what she thought were wild dreams. Someone was chasing her – someone menacing. She ran along the inner perimeter of the manor where the impervious walls offered no escape. Several doors seemed promising, but each was securely locked.

Finally, she reached one with a broken fish lock. She slipped through the door to a familiar setting, but where there should have been stacks of rice, there was instead a row of white pine chests. She heard footsteps of her pursuer. There was nowhere to go, nowhere to hide. One of the chests, wide-open like a cavernous mouth, seemed to invite her in. She climbed inside and lay down with the lid over her, like a coffin.

In the darkness, all her other senses were heightened. The muffled voices were incoherent, but increasingly loud in pitch and intensity. Meanwhile, the box closed in on her, squeezing her tightly. She wanted to scream, but no sound came from her open mouth. The only sound came from outside, but soon there was clarity in the distressed voices.

"No, it can't be! Please, I beg you."

"Woman, let go of me!"

"Have mercy, he is only a boy. Please, please … I beg you…"

Ji-nah's eyes fluttered, struggling to open. She was dreaming in her darkened room. She tried to move her body, but it was like a heavy corpse. She fell back asleep, sinking once more into the wails of commotion.

CHAPTER 16

Off in the distance, too far for a stone's throw, yet close enough for the rattling chortles to reach Han's ears, the magpies teased and mocked incessantly. At least, that's what it sounded like to him as he dusted off the altar table. The singing birds and cloudless blue skies were in stark contrast to his dark mood. Ji-nah lay suffering with chills and fever after the beating he should have borne, and the world didn't seem to care a fig about it.

As soon as she was well enough, he would tell her about his theory on the master's seal. It was all he could think about after his talk with his mother. He still could not reason why the master would board a ship, but finding the tutor with the master's seal might explain the will – that it may not be authentic. How could the master have signed the will with his unique chop, if the tutor had it in his possession?

It was very likely a forged document.

Han bid his time, waiting for Ji-nah to come out of her fever. He was certain she would agree to make inquiries at court regarding the master. She would have to write a letter as the master's ward, and he would deliver it. Maybe they will get some answers as to the master's whereabouts. But then again, if the master had fled ... no, he shook the thought from his mind. The master would not have abandoned the court. Ji-nah's guess that it was a secret mission made more sense.

His thoughts raced as he put all his strength into buffing and polishing the bronze ware. His mother was intent on preparing the best *jesa-sang*, the altar table, to appease the spirits that watched over the manor. She worked in a frenetic pace, looking over her shoulder, constantly afraid of what the tutor might do next.

By early afternoon, the altar table for the mistress and child was ready: pyramid of pears, platters of sweet rice cakes, a string of dried jujubes and persimmons, and a flask of wine. Fresh incense sticks were laid next to the urn.

His mother struck a match and lit an incense stick. She blew it out and stuck the smoldering prayer stick in the urn filled with a mix of rice and sand. She bowed three long times. Cook followed next and then it was Han's turn. By the end of the first day's memorial, there were more than a dozen prayer sticks lit in the urn. The smoke of their prayers rose up to the spirits – day and night, they would keep the incense burning, keeping vigil.

The tutor returned cheerful, as if relishing a delicious secret. He nearly danced around Han, who was sweeping the courtyard. When the tutor noticed the bounty of the altar table prepared on the open verandah, he stiffened. He looked as if he was ready to launch into complaint when Cook rushed out from Ji-nah's room, begging the tutor to fetch a doctor.

"What is her condition?" he asked.

"Fever rages," she answered.

"Fevers are known to break after three days. Why not wait until then?"

Stingy goat, Han thought, but he also suspected it was more than money that kept the tutor from calling a doctor. People would talk if the town doctor found out that the caretaker had savagely punished the manor's ward. No doubt the tutor wanted to avoid gossip, perhaps even wait long enough to give the unsightly wounds on her calves a chance to heal.

"But –" Cook tried again.

"Give it time," said the tutor, waving his hand. "Besides, you said she was stirring."

Cook backed away, bowing as she cowered away like a beaten dog. Since Ji-nah's punishment, everyone was cautious, even the gruff Cook.

The tutor was giddy again when he called for Han.

"I have some news that should please you."

Han looked up from his sweeping.

"You've always wanted to learn." The tutor gave a wolfish grin. "Well, this morning, I made some arrangements."

His mother, carrying a fresh wash bowl for Ji-nah through the courtyard, heard enough to pause.

"What arrangements?" she cried. "You promised he would not be sold!"

"That's right, I'm getting no payment for him." He smiled. "He will not go to another household, and he will not be a slave. My arrangement is better."

"What have you done?" she asked.

"He's always wanted to learn," he repeated. "Now, he will get his chance. With the foreign devils!"

"No, it can't be! Please, I beg of you," his mother cried, dropping the wash bowl and throwing herself at the tutor's feet.

"Woman, let go of me!" the tutor shouted.

"Have mercy, he's only a boy. Please, please ... I beg you," she wailed.

Before the sun went down, Han found himself once again trailing behind the tutor's now crisp, new, linen robes. His own belongings were light on his back. They ambled down the familiar lane, dotted with discarded tracts, torn and trampled, the sullied cross barely recognizable. Meanwhile, the tutor tormented him with frightful stories.

"They steal Korean babies, taking their organs as medicines for their hospitals."

"They consider the eyes a delicacy among the missionary tables." The tutor was enjoying himself.

Jejang.

How could his fate be any worse than serving Tutor Lim? The barbarians didn't scare him – only the thought of leaving his mother and Ji-nah with a monster like the tutor.

They reached an unfamiliar neighborhood situated on the other side of the market area and across the footbridge where a stretch of low thatched huts lined the stream. The lanes were wider, flanked by homes with tiled, curved roofs, much like their own manor, only smaller. They were within view of the double-roofed guardhouse atop the three stone arches – the main palace gates.

But awe of the palace wasn't what made Han's legs feel thick and slow all of a sudden. It was the prominent cross that hung on the truss of a red brick house. They were headed unmistakably toward it.

The frightful cross. How could he expect the spirits to protect his mother and Ji-nah with his clear betrayal? With each dreaded step, he begged for forgiveness to the mistress and child.

Oddly, there was no gate that led into an open courtyard, as one would find in a *yangban* house. Instead, there was only a door, a simple, solid piece of wood that served as the only separation between the golden-haired man who stood inside his living quarters and the passersby outside.

"Ah," declared the missionary man, "my new pupil!"

CHAPTER 17

Small rivulets of water ran from the wet cloth on Ji-nah's forehead, making pools in her ears. The cold tickle stirred her awake. She opened her eyes and met the cook's big, round, moon face.

"You're all right." Cook gave a wide, gaped-toothed smile.

Ji-nah wiped the water from her ears before she tried to get up, but her legs felt like heavy stumps.

"Don't move," said Cook. "Your legs are bandaged."

The mere mention of her legs brought fresh pain. The thick scored rod the tutor shoved into Amah's resisting hand must have cut deep into her calves, but she didn't cry during the punishment. She remembered biting her lip so hard, thinking she'd rather chew off her lip than let the tutor have the satisfaction of breaking her down. The searing pain of the first lash turned to numbness after several more, and she couldn't recall what happened next. She must have fainted.

"Where is Amah? Han?" she asked.

Cook turned aside and rose suddenly. "I'll fetch some broth."

Ji-nah stared at the ceiling, wondering how her home had turned upside down. How was it that she, the ward and proprietress of the manor, lay here wounded by the very guardian entrusted to protect her? How could the master allow this to happen?

She stared vacantly, thinking about the letter Han had shown her in the storage room. Everything started to flood back – the master's mysterious trip to America when the court had not sent him. The stolen letter was evidence that pointed to the logical conclusion – the master had fled. But it was absurd. It was impossible to believe the master a coward. Did tigers have spots?

The last person to see the master was the runner who brought the two letters. She closed her eyes, wondering if there was a way to find the runner with the purple mar and reedy voice. The brazen boy who stared at her when she spoke. The one who was too clean to be a street urchin, and too cheeky to be a coolie.

She tried to think of everything about that day when the runner brought the news. If the master was not sent by court, where was he heading? She couldn't make inquiries to the court, not when the court fine seemed to condemn the master. She needed to speak with Han. There was something else he seemed to want to say before the tutor found them out.

Amah opened her bedroom door with a tray of food.

"Ginseng broth," she said. "It will revive you."

Ji-nah's calves were tightly bound with poultice that had stiffened and made her legs feel like dead tree limbs. She used her elbows to raise herself up.

Amah uncovered the lid off the soup bowl. Steam and aroma rose. She fussed over the small dishes of *banchan* on the tray, still unable to look at Ji-nah.

Ji-nah took her nursemaid's fidgety hands. "It's all right. None of this is your fault."

Amah raised her face slowly. Her red-rimmed eyes were barely visible beneath the puffy folds. Ji-nah squeezed her hand, but the woman burst into bitter wails.

"Han's sold," she sobbed. "After what I did to you, that cheat broke his promise."

Ji-nah's mouth hung open and for a few moments she had no words. The tutor had no honor. "Who would dare buy Master Yi's servant?" she finally managed to say.

Amah stopped her sobs long enough to shake her head and wave her hand in the air as if to break a hex.

"The foreigners?" Ji-nah asked.

The woman nodded, dabbing her eyes with the long tie of her jacket.

The situation was worse than Ji-nah could have imagined. If Han were sold to another *yangban* family, it might be possible to bring him back. But foreigners? Who could reason with them?

"Where's my sense?" Amah said. "Causing you to fret when you need your strength." She spooned some soup and blew on it before she tried to feed Ji-nah like an infant. Ji-nah took the spoon from her and took a sip.

"Boram says he will look out for Han," said Amah.

So the news had spread already. "How could *Boram* look out for Han?"

"The boy says the foreigner passes out rice in the market square, and maybe he will bring Han with him. But what can we do?" Amah sighed. "Well, at least the altar table is prepared. We kept tradition despite everything."

Tradition. The master had never missed the mistress and child's memorial as far as Ji-nah could remember. He always made sure to honor their special day, and unlike the dastardly tutor, the master kept his word. If the court did not send him to America, then there was some other reason. Maybe something or someone kept him from coming home.

CHAPTER 18

Han didn't know where to take his shoes off, but it seemed as if the white man's custom was to keep them on in the house. In a brazier built into the wall of red bricks, a fire crackled, giving off scant heat. The floors were not heated like the manor, where the flues from the cooking fire ran beneath the floorboards, keeping the rooms warm and cozy. No wonder the man kept his shoes on.

The elevated furniture, which he called chairs, also seemed to be balking at the cold floor, for the seats were perched on long skinny legs.

"I only just started the fire. The room will warm quickly," the man said, rubbing his hands rapidly. In the room, he seemed calm, different from the shouting preacher in the public square.

"Ah, where are my manners?" said the man, thrusting his hand out and squeezing Han's in his own large bony hand and shaking it up and down. "It's our way of greeting," he said. "I'm John Abbott."

John patted Han on the back as if he were an old acquaintance rather than a servant he had purchased.

"I'm Han, your servant," he said with a stoop, but the man began to laugh as if Han made a joke.

"Never mind." John waved a hand. "I suppose you're in the dark about the whole affair. I may look as if I need all the help

I can get, but I don't need a servant. It's only my wife and I in this house, and I didn't buy you in the traditional sense. Only that miserable man claimed you were a fetching worker and was relentless in trying to sell me a slave. I suspected he wanted to put you in a wretched situation. So, I guess you can say I did buy you, to take you off his hands. But not to put you in chains again."

Han had no idea what the man was talking about. Between his coarse pronunciation and his odd mix of words, the man made very little sense. Chains, what chains?

"My wife and I are missionaries and we work for the Lord and we bring good news to heathens," the man continued. "So, you see, we are servants, too. But our master is a good Master and we are free slaves."

Han stared blankly and nodded. Who knew what kind of violence the foreigner was capable of if Han disagreed with him.

John sat down on the chair and gestured for Han to sit on the other across him. Han followed tentatively, not daring to look directly at the man, but stared instead at the now roaring fire that spat and blazed. A fire in the living quarters, what a strange custom.

Above the built-in brazier was a tall wooden cross.

Jejang.

"The cross," said John, following Han's gaze. "It's the symbol of our faith. We'd like to offer you a place to stay for your help with the ministry. Then again, you're also free to go. I hold no one against their will."

He dared look at John to see if his offer was genuine, not some trickery. Though the man's features were awfully angular, his face was peaceful and there seemed to be no deceit behind his large, bespectacled eyes. Han bowed, deciding that it would be best to leave the cursed place. Perhaps he could offer his services at the teahouse, work there until the master returned. At least he would be in a better position to hear the news, any news that might help him understand the master's whereabouts.

Outside the front door, footmen declared a formal arrival. John skipped out of his chair and in a flash the door opened, exposing the street.

Four palanquin bearers lowered their poles and opened the screen to the sedan. By the looks of the red and gold trim, it looked to be a palace palanquin. Alighting from the sedan was a fair-skinned, western lady. When she straightened, she was barbarically tall. However, her delicate features resembled a native, with high cheekbones and shrewd, almond-shaped eyes. She was lovely. John took the lady's hand to his lips. When Han cleared his throat nervously, the lady retrieved her hand and turned to Han.

"Are you the new apprentice?" she asked in his native tongue.

Han bowed then quickly remembered that Westerners used their hands to greet. As John had shown him earlier, he thrust his right hand out, grabbed hers, and shook it up and down, stopping short of bringing it up to his own cracked lips.

The lady laughed, showing all her teeth. His shock seemed to prompt her to cover her mouth with her other gloved hand.

What did these foreigners find so amusing?

"John must have taught you how we greet," she said, looking over at the man. The two smirked like a pair of conspirators, making him feel foolish. Unfortunately for them, their entertainment was leaving.

"Han, this is Grace, my fair bride. She's just returning from the palace."

So, it *was* a royal palanquin. What kind of an important person was this lady?

"Gracious, our poor manners," said Grace. "Did you offer Han any refreshments, John?" She turned to Han. "You *will* be staying with us, won't you?" It was less of a question than a sweet demand. Han nodded slowly, bewitched by her sparkling blue eyes and honeyed voice. What kind of trickery had he fallen into? He hoped the spirits would understand.

CHAPTER 19

With fresh scabs, Ji-nah's wounds were healing quickly with Cook's constant attention and herbal wrappings. She was no longer confined to her room, although she was in no condition to return to the servants' quarters to kneel with her sewing. She would remain in the inner house and convalesce.

The time spent alone was good, giving her soul a chance to quiet down and concentrate on a plan. After Amah told her what Han had found in the tutor's possession, things started to make more sense. The court fine, the man in black, and the tutor's possession of the master's seal all indicated some kind of foul play – but there was no clear link. She contrived a letter in her mind. She would send a letter to the court incriminating the tutor for theft and forgery. But, first she had to collect the evidence.

Hobbling along the corridor, she found herself at the entrance to her master's study, now occupied by the tutor. She announced herself at the door and waited. She announced once more, but still no answer.

She ventured to enter. She had the right to her master's books, yet her heart was racing wildly when she slipped into the room. The study had a faint scent of her master's tobacco. She inhaled, taking a deep breath, but the scent was gone. The room she remembered was in disarray – not messy necessarily, but familiar objects were no longer in the same place as she remembered. The room was dusty, neglected since Han had gone, and Amah and Cook were busy caring for her recovery.

What a sorry sight. How quickly things fall apart.

Next to the stained bolsters, where the master once rested his arms, her eyes fell upon a chestnut-colored letter box. She leaped toward it, ignoring the pain in her legs from the sudden jerk. Unable to bend her legs, she stooped at the waist. The chest was locked, but she noticed a familiar purple strand caught in the hinge.

The wooden floorboard in the hallway gave a sudden creak, making her jolt. The door slid open almost immediately, and the tutor stood frozen at the entrance.

"What are you doing here?" he demanded.

"I came for books." Her mouth was dry as cotton.

He moved toward her with a fixed stare, like a snake ready to strike its prey.

"The master said in his letter that he found comfort in *The Annals*," she said. Where the thought came from, she did not know, but her quick thinking seemed to buy her credibility.

"But the bookcase is over there," he said with suspicion, pointing his switch to the other side of the room .

"It looks in disarray. The master used to keep some of his treasured books by his desk," she said, limping cautiously over to the bookcase.

Her labored movement seemed to illicit sympathy for he lowered his switch and offered help. "Let me find it for you."

He fingered through the assortment on the shelf. "Ah, yes, here it is." He pulled it from the shelf and leafed through it. "It's an esoteric work and your master is right for once. There is wisdom in the classics. Like the seasons that repeat their cycle each year, the number four has significance in this work, even if the number itself sounds too close to death. I believe it's deliberate – like the seasons, there is a cycle to death and rebirth."

He handed the book to Ji-nah, but when she took it in her hands, he did not let go.

"Next time, enter this room only when I am here," he said, with fresh menace. He released his grip on the book after she nodded in agreement. She took the book with both hands, trying to ease the shaking. Then cautiously, she made her way out, feeling the hairs rise on the back of her neck.

When she reached her room, she realized she had been holding her breath. She shook all over again, thinking what might have happened if he had caught her trying to open his letter chest. Thank goodness for her quick thinking. She looked at the book in her hand. The master had referred to this tedious book in his letter. It was an odd choice, but now that she held it in her hand, she studied it with care.

The Annals chronicled the Han dynasty's history in fours – birth, follies, triumphs and death – only to be repeated in another season. It read like a poem.

There seemed to be a striking resemblance to the structure of the poems and the letter from her master. She pulled out the letter once more. The odd structure and unusual line breaks. It was indeed, a poem! She examined the letter, then *The Annals*, and back again at the letter. Then she saw it.

Dearest Ji-nah,

*I have not **kept** my promise to return sooner.*
*China, a great **host** nation, has given us security*
*in this past **age**. I have done*
*all my duty **in** China and take the Hinomaru*
*to America via **Japan**.*
*Please, you must **not** worry.*
*Instead, you must **trust** your tutor*
*and listen to **Lim**. When I finish my*
*service to our **queen**, I promise to*
*return safely. Be **in** good spirits and let not*
*these times of **danger** keep you from*
*your studies. Must **go**.*
*I will return **to** the manor, Fate willing and finish my*
*duty to the **court**.*

Lastly, the classics, like the Annals of the Four Seasons will be a
guide to solving all matters.

I write this with my own hand.
Yi Yong-Gi

As if each fourth word in the stanza was illuminated, the words strung together formed a cryptic message. Her master was kidnapped, and the tutor was somehow involved! Her intuition was correct. The master would never put Lim in charge unless he was coerced.

She tried to piece together the tutor's oddities: his support of Taewongun, the master's enemy, and his association with the man in black, who stole the manor's rice. Master Yi was kept hostage in Japan – could it be that the burglar in black was a Japanese mercenary as Han suggested? But why? What did Tutor Lim's selfish gains have to do with Taewongun and a Japanese mercenary? Whatever it was, the tutor was involved in something subversive, something larger than himself. After all, the queen was in danger.

Ji-nah closed her eyes and rubbed her pendant. What was she to do? How could she rush to court when they have essentially fined and condemned her master?

The door slid open and Amah brought in her midday meal. Perhaps her nursemaid could help. Ji-nah read the cryptic message and explained that Tutor Lim was involved in the master's kidnapping. She also divulged her own suspicion that the tutor must be working with Taewongun because the queen was in danger.

At the mention of Taewongun, Amah shuddered.

"What's wrong?" Ji-nah asked. But the woman remained silent.

"Well, the master wants me to go to court, but who will believe me when Master Yi is discredited for avoiding a summons?"

"There's a way," said Amah finally, with a grave expression that betrayed her fear. Amah looked over her shoulder, making quite certain they were alone, and in a hushed voice, said, "You're not who you think you are."

CHAPTER 20

Attached to the red brick house was the print shop where an iron apparatus with long jutting levers cranked up a flat, heavy weight. It was called a printing machine and the white men had brought it from their country. John explained that this printing press was the reason for the spread of Christiandom, his religion, and that it was the Christian mission to teach people.

"That way folks can read the good book for themselves, and not be enslaved by ignorance," John had said.

Han couldn't believe the foreigner actually wanted people to learn their letters. Learning was the privilege of the elite and belonged to those of leisure, not common folk. But the foreign ways intrigued Han, who was starting to wonder how barbaric these people really were.

John said the printing press paid for all the rice they distributed to the poor. They'd run off circulations for officials and foreign legations, but mainly, they used it to run off hundreds of tracts. Hundreds? *Jejang*. As if one cross wasn't enough.

Presently, two Korean boys were operating the clunky levers. They stopped to bow to John, and when they saw Han, they gave a little nod. On the other side of the apparatus, an older foreigner sat laboring over a wooden carton. He picked his way through the box, rattling its contents. He pulled out small blocks, one at a time, placing them on a broad tray.

"That's Henry Goodfellow." John gestured to the old man in the corner. "He's composing another tract." The man set down the tray and looked up over his spectacles. "Is he the new apprentice?" he asked in Han's native tongue.

"Indeed," said John. "Henry, this is Han. Han, Henry Goodfellow."

The stout old man sprang up from the bench with more energy than his silvery white hair and whiskers suggested. His heavily hooded eyelids and wrinkly jowls gave him the appearance of a lazy old tortoise. Certainly, he was twice the age of John, but there was no appearance of deference on John's part. Old men were treated with reverence in Han's custom, but these two shook hands and patted one another on the back with ease and familiarity.

As Han pondered what he'd seen, Tutor Lim's words rang in his mind. *Eum-Yang principle: east is for the East, the west for the West.* The lack of respect was clear from John's treatment of his elder. How could he make this poor old man stoop over a box of blocks?

Han watched the Korean boys who resumed their work at the press machine. They did not look mistreated. By their darkened skin, they looked to be cleaned-up street boys, lucky to have shelter and food the foreigners offered. Han had heard of such people – rice Christians, who embraced the foreign god for a bowl of rice.

"Henry is our language scholar," John interrupted Han's thoughts. "But he could use some help. While Grace and I do speak a fair bit, we don't yet have the skills to set type to the written language."

The short old man displayed the divided box containing blocks etched with *Hangeul* script.

"You look like a sharp lad, and I could really use help." He pointed to his spectacles. "Old and tired eyes." He picked up a block, showing the engraved font. "The trick is you have to set it backwards, so it will take some time to get used to."

Han gulped, wondering how he got himself into this predicament. He could scarcely read proficiently when the type was set forwards, and now he had to read it backwards?

Soon enough he was left with the boys and the old man in the print room. The spritely old man remained impossibly patient despite Han's many faulty steps. After several days' training, Han still took more than two hours to typeset half a line. Henry didn't scold him, nor did he cuff Han's ear for the mistakes on the setting. He wasn't used to such patience, or kindness. For the first time since he'd left the manor, Han didn't feel quite so bad.

He barely had time to think of the manor he'd left behind, although when his eyes weren't swimming in blocks and letters, his heart ached, thinking of his mother and Ji-nah under the vile tutor's hand. He wanted to work hard, prove to the old man he was worthy, then maybe he'd allow Han privileges, like a visit to Boram to get news of the manor. He hoped his mother and Ji-nah were safe, but with every tract Han helped produce, he wondered if he was stirring the wrath of the house spirits.

"*Jejang,*" he muttered.

"Why do you always swear like that?" asked Yong-jin, one of the dark boys.

The three boys were taking a break, slurping noodles from their bowls. Han hadn't realized he had spoken aloud. He didn't need to explain himself, but he didn't want the boys to get the wrong idea that he was some uncouth, foul-mouthed boy.

"Well, I don't exactly have a reason to celebrate my luck," Han said.

"Words have power, you know," said Won-jin, the other, silent boy with a thick tongue.

"How's that?" said Han. The boys quietly ate from their bowls, ignoring him. He would have let the slight go, but how dare they instruct him? What did they know? Words having power indeed!

"You know nothing of my lot," said Han. "I was taken from my family and sold to foreigners, to do this – print crosses, which will only offend my house spirits that are supposed to protect my mother and the family I serve, so 'curse it' seems fitting, doesn't it?

"And do you two even know what's happening in the kingdom? Foreigners are stirring trouble. Don't you know our countrymen are fighting to preserve our ways, and here we are helping the foreigners?"

The darker of the two boys wiped his mouth with his sleeve after setting his bowl down. "Won-jin is my twin," said Yong-jin. They weren't identical, but Han saw their resemblance. "For years, he couldn't hear because our master beat him far too many times. We ran away, living in the streets, begging and picking through trash until these missionary people took us in. Mr Abbott gave us food and clothes but it was the lady, Mrs Abbott with her tinctures and magic hands who opened Won-jin's ears. It was a miracle."

There were shamans who beheld such power, and it struck Han that there was something unusually enchanting about Grace Abbott. "Is she a sorceress?" asked Han.

Yong-jin shook his head. "A gifted doctor, she calls herself. She would be furious if you attribute her powers to witchcraft. She's a Christian."

For the past few days, it had taken Han all his concentration to place the right lettering on the plate that he never bothered to comprehend what the words meant. He paused then asked, "So are you Christians?"

Won-jin nodded his head with vigor while Yong-jin said carefully, "I don't know what all this means, but the Christians feed us, clothe us, and give us power we never had before. All we had to do is say we believe in their God."

"Power? What power?" Han was incredulous that two street boys could possess any kind of power. They weren't *yangbans*, and they'd never be no matter how much they stuffed themselves with rice.

"Hope." The word rolled off Won-jin's heavy tongue.

"*Jae –*" Han stopped himself when the door knob rattled open. Henry ushered in a red-faced Boram.

"Boram?" Han was afraid his friend's antics had landed him in trouble with the foreigner.

He rushed to his friend.

"You're alive!" cried Boram. "I wasn't sure he'd take me to the right place, but I explained to them that I really needed to find you. That man, the old one, has good command of Korean. Far better than the scary, young one in specs!"

Han laughed, recalling his own surprise at the foreigners' command of their language. "What brings you here? Is there any news of Master Yi?" he asked.

"If only it were good news. But I think this is urgent."

Boram slipped a note to Han. It was in Ji-nah's hand:

Run away to the teahouse, if you can. There's evidence that M is in danger. L is responsible and it's bigger than we thought.

Did Ji-nah think that he needed saving from the foreigners? If the master was in real threat, did she think he would sit idle at the teahouse and protect his own hide? No, there's nothing he could do from the teahouse. He thought of the royal palanquin and the fair-skinned lady with healing powers. This was the place to stay if they needed help. Before anyone could read it, Han tore up the note and told Boram, "Tell her I'm staying. I am treated well as you can see."

CHAPTER 21

AMAH

How shall I start?

The Mins are a powerful clan, but they have an equally powerful enemy – Taewongun. You know that name, because it's the name of the queen's enemy, and out of allegiance we do not speak of it. But we also don't speak of that name because it is the name of a wicked murderer.

It was almost fourteen years ago when I lost Han's father – the same fateful day the master lost Lady Yumi, his wife. They both died by the same hand.

The manor was in chaos, as often is the case with a new birth, but especially because the birth was a taxing one for the lady. Nonetheless, the child was healthy and Lady Yumi survived the ordeal, but she was left weak and flagging in appetite. It was still a happy occasion, and messengers delivered gifts from all the *yangban* families – rice cakes, bolts of fabric, ginseng. Naturally, we were all busy tending to her and the newborn. So busy that we thought nothing of a gift that bore no name.

It was a box of dried persimmons, a delicacy and the lady's favorite. It just so happened to be my husband's favorite, too. Like I said, she didn't have much of an appetite, but when she saw those persimmons, she perked up. Generous woman that she was, she took some for herself and gave the rest to Han's father. That night both she and he grew violently ill. By morning, both had died – poisoned.

What a tragedy! Your first day was also your mother's last on this earth. The master, though grieved, bound us – me and Cook – to secrecy. He knew the danger associated with the Min name. So, after Lady Yumi died, he destroyed everything bearing the Min name – including the baby. He led everyone to believe that, too, for soon we were holding a ceremony for three deaths. As instructed, Cook and I hid the infant in our quarters, until of course, as "fate" – really the Master's plan – would have it, an abandoned child mysteriously appeared at the gates of the grieving house. It was a sign from heaven and the master took the child in. That's the official story he had us commit to memory.

Yes, we knew the dried persimmons were from Taewongun. He'd been trying to strike at the Min clan in order to weaken the queen. So yes, all of this, this pretense, was for your safety.

No, the master wasn't trying to deny your identity. He had to pretend because your mother was no ordinary Min. She was smart and beautiful, but for her pale blue eyes – unnatural for a Korean. People called it ghost eyes. Bad luck, they said. But your father isn't like everyone else. He refused to believe in the superstitions, so he lived with a Min far away from court.

But I don't know. I think those ghost eyes did bring bad luck. Look what happened to her.

The name you bear is dangerous. You are a Min, a kinsman of the queen. You have a right for an audience, but I'm afraid you may not be believed.

Why? Because everyone believes that you and your mother perished. The elaborate funeral we held to keep the threat of

Taewongun away from you. The court knows nothing of your existence. That's the challenge.

But you must keep this quiet. If the tutor catches on that you're a Min, and if you're right about him working with Taewongun, then you're in greater danger than you think. He must never, ever find out who you really are.

CHAPTER 22

Ji-nah was still reeling from what Amah had told her. Her father was Master Yi, and her mother a member of the Min clan that made Ji-nah a kinsman to the queen. But what did any of that mean if no one knew of her existence? She squeezed the pendant in her hand and wondered if it belonged to her real mother, Lady Yumi. She forgot to ask Amah. But even if the pendant didn't belong to her dead mother and it was only a part of some contrived story, she didn't want to know. The pendant gave her comfort and a connection to something that had felt like kinship for her over the lonely years.

It was a fantastic story, all too much to take in, but even after the story soaked into her, she realized nothing had really changed. The master was still kidnapped, taken hostage, and the queen was in danger. She wished her master – father – had told her earlier. What harm could have come to her under his protection? But the master's own predicament gave her pause about the danger surrounding the Min name. After all, wasn't he was kidnapped for serving Queen Min?

The name you bear is dangerous.

The threat to her own safety meant little because as far as anyone was concerned, the real Min child had died. Ji-nah was an orphan nobody. Could she convince the queen of such an outlandish claim as to be her kinsman? What proof could she possibly give other than Amah's story? She had the master's letter, and perhaps that was enough. If she could find an ally in court who would consider his cryptic letter, then the tutor would be found out, and the master saved. If only it could be that simple, she may not even need to prove her own identity.

But first, she needed to get to the palace without the tutor's knowledge.

The rest of the afternoon quickly faded into early evening as she prepared her escape. She would travel to the palace at night by foot. She hadn't been outside the manor walls since her seclusion started almost six years ago, but Amah gave her clear directions with landmarks. Amah also supplied her with Han's clothing to disguise herself as a servant to leave the manor. It was only a matter of time before the tutor retired and the house quiet, before she would make her escape. Amah later slipped into her room. Together they said a prayer to the house spirit before they prepared Ji-nah's disguise. Before they could finish loosening Ji-nah's pigtails, there was a loud call from the front gate.

A night visitor at this hour?

Within minutes, Amah had found out who it was and rushed back to her room. "The queen's attendant is here and she wishes to see you!"

Ji-nah couldn't believe her luck. She wouldn't have to sneak away to the palace after all, the queen's attendant was here to come to her rescue! Ji-nah clasped her pendant and thanked her mother's spirit.

"This may be our chance," said Amah, echoing her thoughts.

Ji-nah fixed her hair, tucked the pendant back to her bosom and went to meet her savior.

The face was not what she expected of a warm liberator. Instead, waiting at the seat of honor in the study was a stern-faced lady with all the frostiness of Mount Sorak in winter. Ji-nah bowed, kneeling deep so her forehead touched the floor. She raised her head, but kept her eyes lowered.

"Deepest apologies for the delay, Kim Sanggung," said the tutor. His feeble voice came from the corner of the room. "She is the arrangement we spoke of … I believe you will find her more than suitable."

Sanggung? A high-ranking lady-in-waiting? And arrangement? She remembered Lady Cho and her interrogation. Was this another one of his meetings? Did the queen's lady-in-waiting find suitable matches for the princes in court? She wasn't entirely sure about such matters, but this stern-faced lady had a detached coolness about her, as if she detested being called to such a place at night, that Ji-nah hardly thought this was a match-making interview.

"She has kept me waiting," the lady said. "This does not bode well." Quiet but deliberate, her words had an edge.

"I'm sorry," Ji-nah said. Once more she bowed, letting her forehead touch the floor.

"You have not been addressed," said the lady, then turned to the tutor. "You assured me her manners were impeccable. I've no time for laborious training."

"She has spent just a short time with the servants and is still learning, but she's a good student …" said the tutor.

"Do you know why I'm here?" the lady asked Ji-nah.

Ji-nah actually hadn't thought why the lady would be visiting the manor. In her own excitement to get to the palace and divulge the news of her master's kidnapping, she only assumed the palace attendant was sent by fate. Now she was beginning to see her own folly.

Again, the lady addressed Ji-nah. "You're offered to serve as *nain*. To be of any use to the court, you will have to learn the proper conduct."

Nain? Why, they were practically slaves – the lowliest palace attendants sentenced to serve for life.

"There's been quite a stir in this household," said the tutor, "as you can imagine with Lord Yi absconding and all …"

"Good tutor," said the lady with one hand in the air like the Buddha. "I'm fully aware of Lord Yi's absence. I need not be reminded of your problems when His Majesty's kingdom is in such a fragile state."

"Of course, of course." The tutor's voice wavered. "This girl has much to learn, but I offer her services as recompense for the disgrace of Lord Yi's abandonment. This should settle the manor's debt owed in court."

So, this was the arrangement – the tutor was paying the court fine by offering the palace perpetual servitude – Ji-nah. She looked over at her tutor to catch his smug grin as he lifted his head from a fawning bow. Ji-nah bit her lip, but she couldn't contain herself any longer.

"Please forgive my forwardness," she said. "But Master Yi did not abscond. He is a faithful servant to His Majesty, King Kojong and serves Queen Min. Months ago, he sent a letter saying that he was sent to America by the court, but I'm quite confident he wrote it under duress."

She felt the stab of her tutor's weighty stare. She averted her eyes from his direction and was ready to pull out her master's letter from her sleeve when the lady put her hand up again and stopped her.

"America? I've heard that preposterous story. With so much turmoil in the kingdom, it sounds like a good excuse to abandon his post."

"He did not abandon his duty," Ji-nah said. "He's in trouble – kidnapped, actually. Taewongun is involved and Tutor Lim is his accomplice."

The room fell loudly silent. She chanced a glance at the tutor, whose eyes sparked with murder. The baffled lady broke the silence with an uneasy laugh. "What a spirited child."

The tutor returned her good humor, laughing nervously. "Spirited child, indeed," he said, nodding in agreement. "She reads too many novels, I'm afraid."

"That's quite an accusation," the lady said, ignoring the tutor's feeble comments. "Pray child, what proof do you have?"

Ji-nah pulled her master's letter from her sleeve and unrolled it before the lady. The lady's eyes scanned the entire letter but she showed no sign of understanding.

"Please look at every fourth word in the text and string them together," Ji-nah said.

The lady took a moment. "So inventive," she said with a sigh. "I'm afraid the elders are right. They say trouble follows a woman with too much knowledge." She carelessly let the letter drop between them.

"Yes, I will agree, but I was at the service of Master Yi, who insisted his ward learn the ways of the *yangban*. But she will learn her position quickly. I'm sure of it." The tutor gave Ji-nah a sly glance.

But Ji-nah couldn't let this opportunity go to waste. If she couldn't persuade the lady-in-waiting here in her own home, how was she to persuade anyone at the palace?

"The tutor has stolen the master's personal seal. In his letter chest, you'll find the master's marble seal on a purple cord," she blurted out, pointing at the brown chest at the edge of the desk. "He has it in his possession because the master is held captive."

"What utter nonsense," said the tutor. "Is it not enough that Lord Yi has tarnished his name, and now you, too, want to continue in that vein?"

Perhaps it was the mention of Master Yi, or the lady's genuine curiosity, but the high palace attendant's tight mouth slackened. "Good tutor, it is a small thing to put this nonsense to rest."

"But surely you don't want to encourage such delusions! Her accusations are insulting enough, but to yield to her demands is like entertaining a spoiled child."

"Pray, indulge *me*," she said. "And let us not waste any more time."

The tutor shook his head and muttered, "Indulgent." He removed a key from the tie around his waist.

The lid adorned with a single crane sprang open. It was completely bare.

Ji-nah felt as if she was falling in one of her dreams, but she did not startle awake. Nothing caught her fall and her hopes obliterated in one fell swoop.

"That is satisfactory," said the lady.

"He has removed it!" Ji-nah cried. "He must have hidden it somewhere. Check the other chest, the drawers – "

"Enough!" The lady's word landed with a thud. "You have much to learn at the palace. Your spirited imagination will not be tolerated." She stood abruptly, looming over Ji-nah like a dark storm cloud. She motioned to her attendant at the door. "Let us go. You have kept me here long enough."

Ji-nah remained stone still, until the lady left the room. She had lost her chance at convincing the one person who had the queen's confidence. How could she ever convince anyone at court if the queen's ear did not believe her? Defeated, Ji-nah rose. The tutor caught her arm just outside the doorway. His bony fingertips dug into her skin.

"So, you think you've figured out my plan? You think you can outwit me?" he whispered into her ear. "No one will believe you. You are an orphaned ward of a disgraced man, and now everyone knows that the Yi name is the same as dung. Meanwhile, I've paid my debts – paid the Japanese for your precious master, and now I'm sending you off to pay for his cowardly act – a perfect ending, I'd say.

"Becoming a *nain* is the best outcome for you. Make trouble for me in the palace, and I promise you, a worse fate will await you here in the manor." He finished his sentence by sliding one finger across her throat.

Part Two

CHAPTER 23

The journey was quiet, but for the rhythmic creaking of the palanquin carrying the lady-in-waiting. Only moments before the night visitor, Ji-nah was preparing her escape to the palace in high hopes of getting the queen's help for her master. Now she was heading there, but under a completely difference circumstance. Her body stiffened with each step, realizing she was marching toward her life sentence. As a lowly slave to the palace, how was she to get help from the queen, especially since she had muddled it with the queen's lady-in-waiting?

She looked back at the manor before the bend in the road. Being secluded within the imposing stone walls for as many years as she had, she hadn't seen this view of the manor from the outside for a long time. It was the grandest estate in the neighborhood for the walls around it stretched the entire length of the lane that housed three residences on the opposite side. Was she never to go back home? It seemed like an impossible thought, but that was what the tutor had arranged for her father's false debt.

She had to let the truth be known about the tutor. Oh, why did she act so rashly? Like a fool, she had fallen right into the tutor's trap. He had played along, acting as if he were reluctant to open the letter box, all the while knowing that he had hidden the incriminating seal somewhere else. Why couldn't she have waited to tell the lady-in-waiting about the kidnapping? Oh, the lost opportunity! Her only hope now was to make an ally, a friend in the palace who could help get her an audience with the queen. Would it be possible as a *nain*?

They had left the manor behind, weaving through the rest of the neighborhood as dogs barked at their approaching steps. The dim light from the lantern bearer in front of the palanquin exposed areas of the city she had only seen in her earliest memories. They crossed the broader streets into the market square, where the hint of garlic and spices lingered in the now closed stalls. Continuing on, they came across a small footbridge that crossed the River Han. A foul odor of sewage and rotting vegetables came off the water, nearly making her retch. She tightened the *durumagi*, the coat that draped over her head, to cover her nose and mouth. Through the small opening left for her eyes, she took in the river's surroundings where small open fires and shadows of lean-tos dotted along the noxious water. She couldn't believe people lived in such conditions. Across the other side of the river, in the direction they were heading, a tall cross stood towering above some lower buildings. *Han was there*, she thought. *What cruelty was he enduring at the hands of the foreign barbarians?*

The tutor had managed to neatly dispose each person that mattered to her in the most spiteful manner: her father kidnapped and publicly disgraced; Han, sold to the frightening foreigners; Amah and Cook would be gotten rid of, too. It was only a matter of time. But she was going to the palace, and though the tutor had in mind to sell her, he did not know that she was a Min, kin to the queen. She was determined more than anything to get word to the queen. She must. Her father was counting on her.

They finally approached the palace gates. The three large stone arches of the main gate were impressive, but they threaded through the smaller arch on the left, avoiding the center one reserved for the king's procession. The palace guards, in their traditional regalia holding pikes, allowed them passage; but alongside them, were other soldiers dressed in Western uniforms and carrying fire weapons.

The palace grounds were sweeping and majestic. Master Yi had told her that it was designed after the Chinese Imperial Palace and had all the grandeur to impress foreign visitors. Columns of standing lanterns were lit along the sweeping stone walkway that seemed to stretch infinitely toward a majestic tower, the Great Receiving Hall, with its tiered roof that fanned elegantly like thin fingers.

The traveling party split at this point. The palanquin bearers and the retinue continued on the walkway, while the huskier of the two attendants took Ji-nah toward the western wall. They headed to the remote corner of the grounds, where a cluster of smaller structures stood.

"Quickly now," the husky attendant ordered, when Ji-nah's footsteps fell behind.

"When will I see Kim Sanggung, the lady-in-waiting, again?" she asked.

"For your own good, not unless she wants to see you."

"I have an urgent message for the queen," she said, hoping she could elicit sympathy from the lower ranked lady. "I was hoping maybe you can –"

The attendant stopped in her tracks and faced Ji-nah squarely. Without a crease on her smooth, full face, the attendant was not much older than Ji-nah. Deep furrows set in her smooth brows when she frowned. "You will stop this nonsense. If you've failed to convince Kim Sanggung, what makes you think anyone else can help you get through to the queen? The queen has enough troubles as it is without some idiot bearing false warnings. My advice is that you stay quiet and learn the ways of a *nain*. Do your best there, and maybe one day you can rise in rank and serve the inner house, but keep up your foolish talk, and you'll be cleaning chamber pots." The attendant hastened her steps, ushering Ji-nah along.

They reached a modest building that was to be her new home. All was dark but for a dim lantern set on the pillar.

"Second Attendant, Second Attendant," the husky attendant whispered loudly.

A hinge creaked and out from somewhere in the dark corridor, a matronly lady emerged in her night jacket. With introductions and instructions, the exchange was complete, and the attendant left Ji-nah to her new superior.

"You're late," said Second Attendant. She was a small woman with a pleasant pear-shaped face, but with thick dark eyebrows that gave her a severe countenance. "We were expecting you hours ago. Never mind. Your quarters are in there." She pointed to a darkened hallway. "You will find your new robes by your bed. Get some sleep. Your duties begin early in the morning." Second Attendant didn't give Ji-nah a chance to ask any questions, and rushed her off to bed.

Ji-nah was exhausted. The shock of the night and the long walk to the palace suddenly caught up to her. When her eyes fully adjusted to the dark room, she realized she stood next to the only unoccupied bedding – right beside the door. A row of sleeping bodies filled the length of the room. She lay her tired body down on the thin mat, feeling the hard floor beneath. Sniffling and wiping her eyes, she was filled with angry frustration, but couldn't afford to feel sorry for herself. The pendant reminded her that she had a duty to her family.

The next morning, she awoke to fits of giggles. Young faces peered down at her. She blinked sleep from her eyes, triggering fits of more laughter from two five or six-year-old girls.

"Leave her alone." The two children retreated. Behind them was an older girl, who looked to be about Han's age. Ji-nah sat up from her bed and looked around the tidied-up room. The four sleeping mats from the night before were folded away.

"We were wondering when you'd wake up," said the older girl. With a square jaw, she wasn't comely, but her friendly, round eyes put Ji-nah at ease. "I'm Hee-sun and these two rascals are Hana and Duri." The smaller of the two hid behind Hee-sun's *chima,* as if she were suddenly frightened of the new girl, but still remained curious enough to take peeks.

"I'm Ji-nah," she said weakly. She looked around for the fourth girl. "I thought I counted four beds last night."

"Right, but you slept in and missed Miwon," said Hee-sun. "She's the *other* girl." The way Hee-sun said "other" made Ji-nah think there was more to the story than Hee-sun was revealing, yet Ji-nah didn't want to appear hungry for gossip.

"Are you as old as Hee-sun?" asked Hana.

"I'm fourteen." Ji-nah smiled.

Her smile seemed to open the floodgates, and soon the two young girls were peppering her with questions. "Do you know how to do the fan dance?" "Can you play the *gayageum*, like Miwon?" "She's really good at it!" "Do you cook like Hee-sun?" "Where are you from?"

The last question hit a raw nerve. *Well, I was sold by my tutor who kidnapped my master – father – and he usurped the title of the manor by forgery.* But before she could reply, Hee-sun said, "Later, girls. You have lessons this morning. Go, quickly, before Second Attendant notices you're late. I'll bring Ji-nah shortly."

Hana and Duri scrambled out of the room, leaving the two older girls. Ji-nah lazily got out of bed and changed into her fresh robes. Her stomach grumbled and she motioned toward the door when Hee-sun cleared her throat.

"Aren't you forgetting something?" Ji-nah must have had a blank look on her face for the girl's eyes widened and her head tilted toward the rumpled blanket and bedding. "There are no servants here."

Ji-nah bent down and folded her blanket easily enough, but the thin mat that she slept on was surprisingly cumbersome to fold.

"Haven't you ever made your own bed?" Hee-sun asked.

Ji-nah's face grew hot, and suddenly none of her words would come out. She shook her head like a scolded child.

"Listen," said Hee-sun. "You're going to have to learn some rules around here. You're a servant. No one is going to do things for you. And another thing – it doesn't matter where you came from, keep your head down."

Hee-sun's instructions were similar to the husky attendant's advice the night before. She was beginning to wonder if she'd ever find an ally.

CHAPTER 24

The morning passed quietly with the two brothers at the press and Han with the box of blocks, but on the inside, Han was anything but quiet. His gut told him that his mother and Ji-nah were in danger, and he doubted all over again his choice to remain with the foreigners. Shouldn't he have gone to the teahouse when he had the chance? Ji-nah seemed to think that it would be a safer place for him. There he wouldn't be offending his house spirits by propagating the missionaries' God. He'd also hear of news amongst his own people. Yet something told him that the lady, Grace, could help. Judging by the frequency of the palanquin bearers to the mission, Grace must be someone influential in court. Otherwise, how could she get so many invitations to court? When he asked the brothers, they merely shrugged.

The brothers didn't seem to care a fig about what was happening outside of themselves – they only did what the missionaries told them to do and got their bellies fed. What cares did they have?

"Jejang," he swore aloud this time. Won-jin looked up from his work, and Han half expected a reproachful sermon, but the thick-tongued boy only lowered his eyes sorrowfully, making Han's neck prickle with shame. He wanted to hurl the box of blocks at Won-jin when the door flew violently open.

Old Henry was holding John up as they staggered into the print shop. With rumpled clothes and mussed hair, the two men looked as if they had been in a brawl. Henry set John down on the bench. His broken spectacles sat crooked on his face and blood oozed from the side of John's head.

The boys sprang into action. When Han returned with some water, the brothers had already brought Grace to the scene. She had with her a black bag filled with an assortment of instruments, tinctures and dressings.

Henry drained the bowl of water Han had brought for him.

Grace gasped. "You have a big gash! Who did this to you?" she asked, cleaning off the sticky blood with a rag. She motioned for Won-jin to put pressure on the wound while she rummaged through her bag.

"No *one* did this to him," said Henry. "A riot broke out, and John and I were easy targets for their vexations."

"I don't like this," said Grace. "Not one bit, Henry." She returned to the wound, pouring some rust colored substance on it before she took to her threaded needle. She stitched up her husband's wound like it was a sock to darn. John winced at first, but seemed not to feel the subsequent pricks by the needle.

"The numbing solution is working," John said, when he saw Han's astonished expression.

When Grace finished dressing the wound, she said to John this time, "I don't like this."

"Their ignorance makes them angry," said John. "We must be patient and keep tending to the flock."

"You're there feeding them every day, and this is how they treat you? By abusing you?"

"Grace, this is what we came for," said Henry. "We are teaching them to read – and preaching the good news, and feeding them."

"It's not working with the masses. Your way simply isn't working," said Grace. "Don't you see? Where the head goes, the body follows."

Han didn't know what she was talking about, but it had something to do with his people and their faith. It seemed the two men were also thinking about Grace's obscure meaning of the head and body.

Finally, Henry said, "We each have our calling."

"Casting pearls before swine, Henry?" Her voice had a biting edge. "Don't you remember how the mob persecuted and killed the Catholics before us?"

"Charity, Grace," the old man said. "We must forgive those who do not know. Our task is great before us, but look at our faithful new brothers!" Henry spread his arm toward Han and the two brothers.

Han wasn't a Christian, he wanted to say, but he didn't think it would be wise to contradict the old man. "Your work in the palace will not go unrewarded, but we must still work with the poor," Henry continued. "Give it time, Grace. Give it time."

Grace opened her mouth to speak, but John held her hand and gave it a kiss. She pursed her lips tightly as if she were resigned, for now.

Then Henry hung his head and prayed aloud. "Lord, thank you for seeing us through persecution. Bless the poor savages. Bless them." He droned on, and as he did, John and the two brothers eventually joined the old man and bowed their heads, too. But Grace stood statuesque, wide-eyed and biting her thumbnail, quietly contemplating in her own way.

When she caught Han staring at her, she lowered her head,

joining the others in prayer of blessings for their persecutors.

They were so docile, these missionaries. Yet, somehow Grace seemed different. She didn't seem the type to run back home to take cover, but instead might have stayed and fought back. Her head snapped back from prayer at the sound of the door.

Boram stood at the entrance holding something in his hand. Because the prayer circle was still going on, he tiptoed over to Han and whispered, "I thought to return this." It was an old, tattered Bible.

At the sound of Boram's voice, Henry said a loud "Amen" and shouted, "Hallelujah, God provides!" He took the book from Boram. "I was afraid it was lost for good in all that commotion, and here He sends his angel!" Henry said, looking straight at Grace.

Boram's face turned scarlet.

Grace smiled widely at Boram, but it seemed disingenuous, an overly exaggerated gesture of gladness to see a complete stranger. "What else may we do for you?"

The attention was too much for Boram, who looked like he would die of embarrassment. He wrapped the long loose tie of his jacket around and around his knuckles and wouldn't speak. Han shook his friend's arm, which seemed to help.

Boram looked around, and when he noticed Grace was cleaning her instruments, he said to Han, "My master, the Cho family … we are leaving. I didn't know when I would get another chance."

"Leaving? Where to?"

"Back to our hometown, Cholla province, like your master." Then realizing his mistake, he quickly added, "I mean Cholla is his hometown, too. Not that your master is there … although people are saying that he fled, but I don't believe it –"

"Who's been spreading rumors?" said Han.

"Your tutor," Boram said quietly.

"Many people in court are leaving," said Grace, surprising Han. "They're afraid to be associated with the king's unpopular decision to side with the West. There might be repercussions in such alliances."

How did this foreign woman know so much about the kingdom's affairs? As if John read Han's mind, he said, "Grace is often invited to the palace ever since she successfully treated the queen's carbuncle –"

"John," she said, elbowing him, "that is a private matter."

Han was beginning to understand Grace's mysterious influence and power. So that's how the magic healer had made her influence into court. Is that what she meant by the "head"?

"I haven't much time," Boram said, interrupting Han's thoughts. "Your tutor dismissed everyone. Your cook is coming with us to Cholla, since she has relations there."

"What of mother? Of Ji-nah?"

"The cook said your mother insisted on staying in Seoul because you and Ji-nah still remain here. She didn't know where your mother went, but Ji-nah, well, she's been sold to the palace as *nain*."

Upon hearing "palace", Grace's ears perked up. "Who is Ji-nah?" she asked.

"She's my master's ward, and the rightful heir to the manor," Han explained. "The tutor – he is a thief." Once Han opened his mouth, his words spilled like water from a broken jug. He told them all about the tutor's betrayal: the beatings, the stolen rice, the letters from court and the possession of the master's personal seal.

He wanted to convince everyone who would listen that the tutor had to have stolen the master's seal and that the master was not a coward who ran away to Cholla. The men listened with growing concern and sympathy.

"We will help find your mother," said John. "And perhaps Grace could make inquires at the palace for your friend, Ji-nah."

A steely look came over Grace's expression. "I have no such influence to ask the queen," she said.

"Surely, you can bring up a small matter such as this," said John.

Grace gave him a look that seemed to make him sheepish for asking. "I have a responsibility to the queen for her good health, physically and spiritually. I do not want to create any undue stress on behalf of a commoner's affairs."

"Master Yi is no commoner. He's an important court official," said Han. He had been wanting to ask for her intervention and this was his chance.

"But you say he is discredited. I do not think it's wise." Then turning to John, she said quietly, "I must gain her trust."

Henry, who had been listening quietly to this exchange, suddenly cleared his throat. He arose from the bench and patted the book that Boram had retrieved.

"One good turn deserves another, Grace," he said. "Sometimes, the head follows when the body moves."

Han didn't understand what the old man meant, but by Grace's dark look, he had said something that hit a nerve. After a pause, she let out a long sigh.

"If the opportunity presents itself, Henry," she said. "I will ask of this Ji-nah from the Yi Manor."

CHAPTER 25

Sometimes it's best to keep quiet about what you know, for no one likes a braggart. It was a lesson she knew, but of late, Ji-nah's impulsive nature had gotten her in trouble.

It was at breakfast when she met Miwon, the other, fourth roommate. Hee-sun said they were the same age, but Miwon was so different from Hee-sun. Superficially, Hee-sun had a sturdy build. Whereas, Miwon had a lithe and delicate frame like a songbird, though her alert, almond shaped eyes and sharp nose were more akin to a peregrine falcon. But more noticeable were her manners.

When Ji-nah and Hee-sun joined the others for instructions with Second Attendant, Miwon turned her jutting chin away from the entrance, refusing to greet the newcomer. While Hee-sun was warm and inviting, Miwon's cool sidelong glance was the kind of reception that Ji-nah did not expect from a lowly servant. The girl, a *nain*, put on airs to match Kim Sanggung, the lady-in-waiting! Ji-nah had never been snubbed before, and the sting of it perhaps made her act rashly.

"Late again," Second Attendant said to Ji-nah, referring to the previous night's late arrival. "I'll make an exception for your first day, but from now on, you will be expected to be here on time as everyone else. You'll learn your letters with us."

A *Hangeul* primer was spread before Hana and Duri, the younger girls, but it looked as if Miwon was learning the basic *Hanja* characters.

"But I already know my letters, even *Hanja* characters," Ji-nah said. The moment the words left her mouth, she realized her mistake by the look on Second Attendant's face. Ji-nah meant to rankle the haughty girl's complacency, but her boast seemed to provoke the wrong person.

"Well," said Second Attendant, "since Ji-nah already knows her letters, it seems appropriate she should learn something she doesn't already know. How do you feel about laundry duty?"

Miwon laughed heartily, yet also daintily like a lady, covering up her mouth. Her manners were so odd that Ji-nah wondered who this arrogant *nain* thought she was.

Not to be outdone, Ji-nah responded, "I would be delighted."

The palace was taking precautionary measures, cleaning and washing almost everything because there had been an outbreak of rat's disease in the city. At least that's what Ji-nah was told by the laundering attendant who seemed relieved for any help, even if it was someone with no training.

That was how later that afternoon, Ji-nah found herself with a paddle in hand, stirring a giant boiling kettle of soiled linens. *What a fool*, she thought to herself. It was a steep price to pay for showing up the haughty girl she barely knew or should care about. It was also petty and beneath her to flaunt her knowledge, but the surprise and envy on the haughty girl's face were worth it. But what had she done? She had fallen in rank before she even began! How would she ever get into the inner court?

She sighed, wiping the sweat that dripped down her forehead. Hee-sun was learning to prepare the *surasang*, the royal table. She wondered if she could eventually ask Second Attendant whether she may learn to cook. Then she might be able to serve the queen.

"I'd scoop that up, if I were you," Hee-sun's voice came from behind, interrupting her plans. She handed her a long, wooden ladle and gestured toward the rising gray foam.

"Hee-sun, I was just thinking about you." Ji-nah took the ladle and scooped up a heap of water along with the floating scum.

"Good thing I came to check on you. Look! You're going to burn the clothes if you don't keep an eye on the water level." Hee-sun took a gourd-full of water and poured it into the roiling pot several times until the bubbles ceased. "Look, I know you're not fit for this kind of job, but you can't be daydreaming. If you do, Second Attendant will assign you to something worse, like chamber pots. What are you thinking about anyway?"

Ji-nah didn't know whom she could trust for help at the palace, and she wondered about Hee-sun. The girl seemed to know Ji-nah was incompetent with simple chores, like bed making, but didn't seem to despise her for it. Instead, she showed her kindly how to do things. It seemed that Hee-sun had a genuine helpful nature – isn't that why the younger girls took to her?

"As you can see, I'm not fit for this job or any job here," she said. "I don't belong here like you. I grew up in a manor. I can read – I'm a *yangban's* daughter. My father is Master Yi and – " She didn't finish her sentence because Hee-sun dropped her good-natured smile and a scowl formed tightly around her mouth.

"A simple thank you would have been just fine," Hee-sun said, then mumbled as she started to leave, "Turns out you're just as arrogant as Miwon."

Here was one person who offered her kindness, and it seemed that Ji-nah only managed to offend her somehow. She had never spoken to girls her age – the only companions she had were Han and Amah, and they were her servants. In that moment, Ji-nah understood her mistake: that she had been speaking to everyone as if she were above them. She didn't realize how arrogant she must have sounded. She wasn't too different from Miwon, after all.

"Wait! I'm sorry, Hee-sun – and thank you," she said. "But I'm nothing like Miwon. It's just that I've never had many friends."

The admission to her weakness seemed to have an effect and a smile returned tentatively on Hee-sun's face. "No, you're not like Miwon … not too much."

Ji-nah laughed. It felt good to have a friend and she was starting to like it. She remembered how her master used to say that patience draws out a person's true nature, and she decided that she would be patient – with herself and her new friend.

"Well, what is Miwon like?" she asked. Gossip seemed natural among friends.

"Miwon? She thinks she's superior to me because she's training to be a lady in court."

"Is that possible?" Ji-nah asked. She thought *nains* trained to be servants, not ladies.

"Not usually. She's got a pretty enough face, and Kim Sanggung noticed her. She's being trained in finer arts like poetry and music. I bet she thinks she can nab the prince or something."

"Is she of noble birth?" Ji-nah asked, wondering if it was enough to have a pretty face to marry into the royal family. What a boon to go from *nain* to concubine!

Hee-sun looked plainly at Ji-nah as if she were a dolt. "She has no connections – she's like us – from poor families happy to be rid of another mouth to feed. No, it's her beauty. People say she looks a lot like the queen. She gets summoned to spend time in the inner court from time to time. That's why she's so haughty. She knows she'll be lording over us soon enough. But don't mind her. Just do your job and be patient. Second Attendant is quite fair. She's a toothless tiger – all roar and no bite."

For the rest of the afternoon, a single thought consumed Ji-nah: *Miwon had access to the inner court.* This thought melted into her mind like a candy in her mouth, giving her hope for the first time since she arrived at the palace. She wondered how she would befriend this girl who despised her. She would have to swallow her pride, she thought. She'd have to, if it meant saving her father.

"*Aigu!*" the laundry attendant yelled, shoving Ji-nah aside. "You've scorched the sheets!"

CHAPTER 26

As if the riots and disruptions weren't bad enough for Henry and John, the rat disease that broke out in Chemulpo, the port city, was creating a wave of panic that reached Seoul. Henry and John seemed truly alarmed when Mr Sill, the American minister from the legation, came harried with an urgent request.

"We must translate this at once, and distribute it widely." Mr. Sill held out a circular in English on hygiene to prevent the spread of the pestilence. "The natives don't have an understanding of cholera. There'll be more riots, mind you, once the disease spreads widely in the capital. They already blame us, the foreigners, because we aren't getting sick. Only the natives are dying from this wretched disease."

After Mr. Sill's dire portrayal of the situation, everyone was on edge and went frantically to work. Han and Henry worked tirelessly to translate and set type to the new circulars. It took several days and long nights, but finally they produced enough leaflets to distribute in and around the market square. John hadn't been out to preach or hand out tracts and rice since his head injury – Grace made sure of that, pulling her rank as his doctor. Now with Mr. Sill's warning, the two men thought it best if the native boys disseminated the circulars. "The people will trust you," they said as they handed them the stacks of freshly inked paper.

Han and the brothers set out for their task. It had been a while since Han had run errands in the city and when they approached the familiar road to the market, he had a sudden ache for his mother. He thought of breaking off from the boys to visit the teahouse, where he was certain his mother was staying, biding her time to collect him and Ji-nah when the master returned. He wasn't sure why, but a part of him resisted. There was the important duty the missionaries had placed upon them, a burden to help their people from getting the disease. But there was something else that nagged at him deep inside his gut. He hated to admit it, but he was afraid to see his mother. So much had happened since he left the manor, so many confusing thoughts he was still muddling through. And though he didn't believe he was a Christian, he felt in some way as if he had betrayed not only the house spirits by helping the missionaries, but also his mother.

They meandered through the winding streets until they reached the market, which looked nearly deserted. It was too early in the day for the stalls to be closed, but many were boarded up with signs that simply had a picture of a rat. The boys put up the circular, pasting them over the rat signs to inform any passersby, and continued through the square, posting notices on wooden pillars and sides of buildings. Their notices warned citizens to keep the ditches from clogging and the well water areas clean.

They traveled together through the heat of the day, handing out paper, informing anyone willing to listen, and teaching the obvious illiterates they encountered on the streets. They made their way toward the river town, where the poorest set up shacks along the banks. The odorous river was the communal fountain and wash tub. Women washed their food and dishes, or beat their laundry against rocks at the edge of the river. Their children dipped in and out of the water, bathing, playing or foraging for their meal. Han spotted a nut-brown twig of a boy wriggling like an eel out of the water. He had dredged up some watercress and was pulling them by the clumps.

"*Ya!*" Han shouted, waving his hand in the air.

The boy, squinting with suspicion, slowly waded over with his green catch as if Han might strike a deal.

"A half-*yang* for the whole bunch."

"I don't want to buy your watercress," Han replied. "That stuff will kill you." He started to explain to the boy about the illness. "Rat disease is not just from rats. You know you can get it from eating vegetables in bad, dirty water."

The boy cocked his head, unsure if Han was speaking the truth or if he was trying to rob him of his watercress.

Han pointed at the foaming pool of scum near the women's washing, a small collection of garbage further on, and a green film of rot gathering near the shallow eddies.

"You see all that filth? That's what's making people sick. Eating watercress that grows in the polluted water is going to kill you."

"But we've been eating it forever."

"When there's an outbreak of the rat disease, you have to be careful. Don't worry, I won't take your vegetables, but do you really want to take chances?"

The boy looked again to where Han was pointing, noticing the polluted water for the first time. He shook his head and turned back toward the other children.

"Tell your friends, all right?" Han shouted.

The boy turned his head and nodded then flung the bunch of greens down the flowing river.

A warm feeling spread through Han's chest. He stood tall and took a deep breath. The lungful of foul air made him gag and cough, but the stench couldn't bother him in a deeper way. He felt good because he had helped someone.

He returned to the two brothers who seemed to be finishing up their talk with the women on the shore. Yong-jin seemed to notice Han's lighter stride.

"Feels good, don't it?" Yong-jin said, as if he understood what had transpired between Han and the swimming boy.

"I think I may have saved his life," said Han.

The brothers smiled broadly. If Han hadn't experienced for himself what it felt like to help someone, he might have cursed those two for their idiotic grins.

"We have a duty to help our people," said Won-jin. "It's our mission."

Mission. The word gave him pause. His duty to educate the people didn't seem like an overbearing one. In fact, the spread of the pestilence made his task seem important, giving him a real sense of purpose and pride. His learning gave him a chance to warn others. For a fleeting moment, he felt like the young boy who played on that boulder, pretending to be an admiral of a ship, filled with urgency and a sense of adventure. He wondered if this good feeling was what made the missionaries feel worthy enough to risk everything and leave their homeland.

As the sun began to cast longer shadows, the three tired boys were ready to call it a day. Hungry and thirsty, the boys headed back, dreaming about food, glorious Korean food they missed so much: spicy pickled cucumbers, cool seaweed soup, and sizzling mung bean cakes with a nice, hot, steaming bowl of pearl rice. The food that awaited them in the mission, however, was for the most part western, not particularly satisfying to their tastes. The Westerners complained about the native spices upsetting their constitution, preferring bland foods. Legume stews or overcooked vegetables soup with rock hard bread was the reality of what awaited them. But to a Korean, a meal never felt like a complete meal unless there was rice.

The brothers might resist straying from their orders, but Han was in such a good mood that he felt daring enough to suggest a visit to the teahouse. They had no money amongst the three of them, but Han offered that they teach the lady at the teahouse in exchange for their meals. The brothers seemed agreeable to the idea and the three went in high spirits down the broad street thinking of the cool soybean soup and other delicacies that might await them.

When they reached the narrow lane, the usual bustle around the entrance was strangely quiet. The welcome lantern that ordinarily hung from the pillar was missing. Even the brothers who had never been to the teahouse sensed there was no sign of life, but Han insisted that they go in. Might his mother be there?

"Auntie!" Han called, pushing the unlatched gate. She wasn't blood relations, but she was close enough to his mother that he called her "auntie" just the same. He called out again as he entered the courtyard. The long wooden tables on the open verandah were cleared and put away. The naked room looked tired and worn with scuff marks exposed on the wooden floor. Even the private dining rooms that were always gaily lit behind the sliding paper doors were eerily dark and quiet as tombs. "Anyone here?" he shouted.

"Who's here?" a voice came from one of the back rooms.

The two boys looked panicked, ready to flee as if they'd heard a ghost, but Han steadied them.

"Auntie?" Han said again.

Tea Auntie came forward with an oil lamp even though there was still light enough in the day. "We're closed," she said, waving her hand as if they were pesky flies.

"It's me!" Han cried. "Is my mother here?"

"Han? Is that you? Why the dumb luck," Tea Auntie said, squinting. "Wait here." She scurried off back into the dark hallway before Han could ask any more.

Yong-jin asked Han, "Are you in some kind of trouble with her?"

Han shrugged.

"Let's go," said Won-jin to his brother. Yong-jin nodded and the two gestured for Han to come along, but he wouldn't budge.

"Go if you must, but I thought patience was a Christian virtue," Han said. It was awkward using an argument he knew nothing about, but there was something important in the Tea Auntie's voice. The brothers shifted uncomfortably as they waited.

What could be keeping her? He wondered.

Floorboards creaked by the shifting weight that shuffled across the long hallway. From the darkened corridor emerged Tea Auntie supporting a haggard figure. The two shapes limped closer toward the boys.

"*Uhmunee!*" cried Han, throwing off his shoes and rushing up to hold up his mother. "What happened to you?"

Han's mother was a sagging heap, but she perked up at the sight of him. "Han! *Aigu!*" she cried, ignoring his questions and hitting his back repeatedly with relief. With her head bandaged and one eye swollen shut, she looked as if she'd been kicked in the face by an ox, but despite her pitiful state, there was a spark of joy before a cascade of tears.

"*Whaa*, your son comes and you perk up so quickly," Tea Auntie teased, trying to cheer up his mother. She turned to Han. "Your mother was in pretty bad shape. That caretaker did this, you know!"

What kind of a beast would beat up a woman? That coward claims he's a *yangban*, too much of a gentleman to mete out punishment to Ji-nah, but he has no reservations about beating up a poor, old and defenseless servant! He remembered his own beating at the tutor's hands, but this was his mother and a different kind of anger burned. He wanted revenge, to make the tutor pay for hurting his mother, but he also felt helpless. Justice always felt denied to the weak and vulnerable. He struggled for words. "I'll get that, that, that – bastard!"

His mother patted him gently now, trying to calm him down as she wiped away the streams on her face with the back of her hand.

"He is pure evil, and he is up to something –" his mother began.

"Shh … " said Tea Auntie. "There will be time enough to explain. First let me get refreshments and we can unfold the stories inside."

The two brothers helped light lanterns and set up tables and cushions in the private dining room while Tea Auntie brought out their meal, apologizing for the scant offerings.

"The rat disease is holding up my suppliers from the port city, so I thought I might as well close shop for a while; and besides, your mother needed tending," Tea Auntie said.

But to the hungry boys, the table set before them was an extravagance. Soy bean soup, chive pancakes, broiled fish, and kimchi – they had a feast, and of course pearl rice made it a proper meal. His mother drank some broth, and insisted they eat without any upsetting talk. He looked up and saw that she was watching him with her one good eye. She sighed as if she had enjoyed the satisfying meal.

"I'm so glad you're all right," she said. "I thought you'd be mistreated." She looked at the two brothers. "You're the barbarian's servants, too?"

The brothers had their mouths full, but after a moment Yong-jin swallowed and said, "They give us food and shelter for work, but they are not barbarians. They do not mistreat us."

Yong-jin's accurate statement surprised Han. The foreigners were less barbaric than their own tutor, a fellow countryman, who savagely beat his mother. He felt the heat of his rage rise again and could no longer wait.

"There's no reason for the tutor to beat you like this. Tell me, what happened?"

She shook her head as if she didn't want the talk to spoil their dinner, but finally her tongue loosened. "The tutor is up to evil," she began again. She started to tell him what happened to Ji-nah and how before she was sent to the palace, she had deciphered the master's letter. "He's kidnapped by the tutor. So I knew he was up to something," she said. "I knew that if I could get my hands on the master's seal, then it would incriminate the tutor. But he caught me."

Han did not like the sound of this and his palms began to sweat. "Did you get the seal?"

"No," she said. "I think he wears it on himself because from time to time, I've seen a purple cord dangling from his breeches. No, he caught me for something else.

"A few nights ago, a stranger came to the manor, and before I could usher him in, the tutor whisked him away to the study. When I brought in some refreshment for the guest, the tutor stood by the doorway and took the tray. I didn't get a chance to see him. But that only piqued my suspicion. I pretended to leave, only I stayed behind and poked a hole through the paper door. Then I saw him. I had seen him before – the eggplant birthmark on his face, who could forget? It was the runner that brought Master Yi's letter."

Han remembered him, too – the boy's arrogance seemed unusual for a servant.

His mother continued, "I listened to them talking and they said something about Taewongun. When I heard that name, I knew it was dangerous, especially since the master's letter said the queen was in danger as well.

"Then I heard the tutor complain about the rice payment for a job unfinished. The visitor said something about Miura Goro being his boss who will give the order. I realized then that this visitor was no runner but a Japanese gang leader of some sort. I must have gasped because they both stopped talking and the tutor came out and ordered the Japanese thug to beat me."

He gnawed on his clenched fist. So, that dastardly snake had the thug beat up his mother!

His mother sensed his fury. "This is nothing – I will heal," she said, "but the information might save the master or the queen herself!"

His selfless mother saw the bigger picture in everything, it seemed. And she was right, of course. The best thing he could do was to stop the tutor's evil plan. The information she got was costly.

"Miura Goro," Han whispered, etching the name in his mind. It was a Japanese name that belonged to a leader. It was becoming clear in his mind: the runner served his leader Miura Goro just as the tutor served Taewongun; they were plotting something; and both his master and the queen were in danger. "What is this order Miura Goro will give?" Han asked.

She shook her head. "I was found out before they said any more."

Han's mind was buzzing, trying to fit the assorted pieces together like the printing blocks. He suddenly had an idea. He thanked Tea Auntie and entrusted her to take good care of his mother.

"I'll come back, Mother," he said. "I think I may have a way to ask the palace for help."

The three boys took their leave, and bowed once more at the gate. Tea Auntie seemed trouble all of a sudden.

"How did you boys get in?" she asked.

"The gate was wide open," Han said.

"Strange." She scratched her head. "I could have sworn I locked it. I'll have to be more careful."

CHAPTER 27

Even in the farthest corner of the palace, news traveled. Gossip or facts, it didn't matter; each tidbit was a glimpse into the outer world Ji-nah had missed all these months without Master Yi. She kept her ears pricked and head down as advised by the husky attendant and Hee-sun, hoping to hear anything that might get her get closer to the queen and help her father. She even sunk so low as to be nice – at least not sour – around Miwon. She was going to need Miwon's help. But despite her kindness toward the arrogant girl, Miwon's response was cool and indifferent. Ji-nah wasn't having any luck gaining the girl's confidence.

It was also disheartening with all the work piled on her. The unusually hot and wet summer brought on the rat disease that had gripped the city. She heard hospitals were set up at the East Gate, but everyone knew that once you went to the hospital, you never came back. Except The Shelter, or that's what people called it. It was a special hospital set up by missionaries on the edge of the city. People said that the infected often returned from the dead, sometimes with a stronger constitution than before their illness. The foreigners had a strong God.

With more work trickling down to her level, she lamented at the sight of her once soft hands, now unrecognizably swollen and rough. Most evenings, she collapsed in bed the same early hour as the younger ones, but tonight when she returned late from starching and ironing, she found Miwon looking at herself in the mirror, taking off her headdress, the heavily braided wig that attendants wore.

Hee-sun, glad to see Ji-nah, excitedly shared her day. "We made *blinis*, Russian pancakes that taste like sweet dumpling skins. They also eat these little finger-shaped savory cakes filled with cucumbers and egg."

"It's not a real meal without rice," said Ji-nah, laughing at the tired, but true, old saying.

"The Chief Kitchen Attendant said that we needed to learn more Western cuisines because foreigners don't have taste buds," said Hee-sun. "I think there's going to be a big party."

"What does a kitchen maid know?" said Miwon smugly from her vanity table.

"Ha!" said Hee-sun. "The Chief Kitchen Attendant said that she's to learn how to prepare these Western dishes because the queen has invited ladies for tea. They're going to open a church – or was it a school …"

"A church? Shows how much you know. The queen wouldn't adopt a foreign god," Miwon said knowingly. The haughty girl's scoffs intended to snub Hee-sun but she also kept an eye on Ji-nah. *Let her boast*, thought Ji-nah. Perhaps she could stoke the haughty girl's ego to get her to help.

"I wonder what kind of ladies will be at this party?" Ji-nah said, hoping to engage Miwon.

"Western ladies – though from which country, I've no idea. They all look the same to me," said Hee-sun, offering nothing new.

Miwon turned aside with a sneer, as if the gossip was beneath her.

"I suppose you'll be attending, Miwon," said Ji-nah. "You're often called upon the inner court. I'm sure the queen will want you by her side."

It was meant to flatter the girl, but it came out all wrong in an unintended mocking tone. Miwon stared coldly at her, as if she knew Ji-nah was angling for something. Ji-nah knew all hope was lost in gaining this girl's help. But to her surprise, Miwon faced Ji-nah and examined her carefully. "Are you the ward of Lord Yi?"

Caught by surprise, Ji-nah was tongue-tied.

The haughty girl turned away again.

"I am," she croaked. "Why do you ask?" She could see the girl's indifferent expression through the mirror.

"Like I said, I hear things," Miwon said.

"What have you heard?"

"Do you know he's disgraced in court?" Miwon continued, looking into her mirror.

"That's not true!" Hee-sun piped fiercely, protecting Ji-nah even though she had no idea what she was talking about. Ji-nah loved Hee-sun for it.

"Lies," said Ji-nah. "Rumors and lies – that's what you're learning in court. I pity you."

"What do I care if you believe me? But Kim Sanggung is not one to lie," she said, turning around now. "The only reason she spoke of it was because a foreign lady asked about you, and Kim Sanggung said not to bother the queen with your inquiry because it would only upset her. Her trusted official has fled the court."

"Why would she say something like that?" asked Hee-sun.

"Because it's true," said Ji-nah, surprising everyone, even herself. "At least partly true. He didn't flee. He's kidnapped." She didn't know why she started revealing everything about the master; it was against her better judgement to blurt out the danger he was in, but Ji-nah desperately wanted to clear her father's name from being repeatedly sullied by gossip. It was like hearing people say that the sky was green. She would at least set things straight with the *nains*. Besides, she had lost all hope in gaining Miwon's goodwill; they were too much alike – prideful and arrogant. The best she could hope for was to tell her the truth about Master Yi.

She told them everything from the day the runner brought the ill news that her master was going to America to the day she was brought here, sold as *nain* as payment for a debt her tutor had trumped up to the court. She told them about the deciphered letter that said her master was kidnapped and that the queen herself was in danger. She told them that the tutor was working with Taewongun and the Japanese, somehow.

She told them everything – except the fact that Master Yi was her father.

For the entire length of the story, Hee-sun's mouth hung open and stayed that way well after Ji-nah had finished. Miwon listened quietly, staring at Ji-nah's hand that had been clutching her pendant. Ji-nah discreetly tucked it away.

"Well, that's a fantastical story," said Miwon. "Kim Sanggung mentioned that you were an imaginative child."

"I'm not that creative," she said. "Miwon, can you help me?" Even to her own ears, her beseeching sounded so pitiful and convincing that Miwon's hardened face seemed to soften. But the arrogant girl shook her head again.

"Do you even know what is happening in court?" Miwon asked, as if reminding herself. "Ever since the Japanese won the war against the Chinese, the Japanese Resident Minister and his soldiers have occupied the palace. The Japanese have strong-armed

King Kojong and forced out the brave officials who have remained and placed instead their spies and cronies in the new cabinet. The queen is in constant danger for her life because the Japanese know she is King Kojong's backbone. There are just too many attempts to weaken the queen and she trusts no one, except her own clan. I can't go in there defending an official who has fled. It would be my own demise."

Ji-nah hadn't heard about the outcome of the war. The two great dogs fighting on their soil had ended with China's tail tucked between its legs. She thought about the tutor and the Japanese prowler in black – the one in cahoots with the tutor. It was all beginning to make sense because the Japanese had won the war and have taken over the palace. Her father, a loyal official to the royal family, would have been replaced if he were not kidnapped. Perhaps her father knew the Japanese would win and the queen's life would be in danger. It was even more imperative that Ji-nah reach the queen. She was a Min, wasn't she?

The pendant seemed to thump against her chest. *Don't ever mention ghost-eyes again. It's bad luck*, she recalled Amah saying. But bad luck or not, those cursed-eyes of her mother made Ji-nah a trusted Min, the queen's kinsman. Ji-nah decided to give away the last secret she had, whispering into Miwon's ear, "Then ask the queen if she knows Min Yumi."

CHAPTER 28

The wispy clouds that streaked the mid-summer sky were an empty promise of rain. A good downpour would wash away the pestilence, or at least alleviate the charge in the atmosphere. The heat and humidity only seemed to enhance the powder keg mood. The once peaceful city was rife with arrests of rioters who called themselves *Donghaks*, his fellow countrymen who wanted to rid all foreigners – Westerners and Japanese.

The Westerners were not as offensive as the Japanese who brought armed soldiers and policemen to their city. Defeating China in the spring seemed to have given Japan the right to move into the Korean kingdom. Aiding the palace guards, Japanese soldiers were picking up *Donghak* rioters and public executions were occurring on a regular basis. Disgraced officials were denounced as traitors and their heads on pikes warned against insurrection. But Han was confused as to who was battling whom. Loyalists to the crown worked against the Japanese while some rival factions aided by Taewongun, sided with the Japanese; and everyone seemed to persecute the *Donghaks*, who wanted all foreigners gone. It was all a mess and Han just wanted peace in the kingdom again. He wanted Master Yi to return to his rightful place and take back the manor, and make sense of the kingdom once more.

Oh, how he wished a good hard rain would wash away all the chaos in the kingdom. For now, the Westerners didn't seem quite as meddlesome. They were helpful in Han's mind. They were helping to slow the spread of rat disease, and The Shelter that was set up by the missionaries was doing more good than anyone expected. The foreigners had some kind of magic the native healers didn't know about, and soon sick folks caught wind and were lining up at their door.

The Shelter needed around-the-clock attention, and when the boys were not in the print shop or distributing leaflets, they were helping to boil water, distribute briny broth and disinfect the hospital with lime. All hands were needed for the row of sick patients. Han had seen Grace, kerchief around her face and hair tied back, carrying tubes and bowls to patients – her black bag never too far – and nursing the dying back to miraculous health.

Other doctors from the missionary field came to help out at The Shelter, relieving Grace. She would disappear for part of the day, making her trek to the palace, it seemed. One morning, before Grace's shift had begun on the floor, Han ventured to ask if she had fulfilled her promise to ask about Ji-nah.

Grace quickly tied her apron and secured her cap and kerchief. Han couldn't see her face, only her beguiling eyes. "As you can see, we are preoccupied," she said.

Han might have let it go, but the danger he pieced together only made matters urgent for the master. "You have promised," he reminded her again.

"The kidnapped nobleman," she said. "I understand your concern, but the queen has enough worries without her physician alarming her. There are things you don't understand." She waved him away dismissively, as if he were nothing more than a street beggar.

"You think I'm ignorant," said Han. His old self might have cowered to this enchantress, but the image of his battered mother gave him courage. "The queen herself is in danger. The same hand that kidnapped my master is working to plot against the queen."

"There are many plots – court intrigue is nothing new," she said, turning away.

"Like yours?" he said.

He couldn't tell how his words affected her, but they were enough to stop her from ending the conversation. She slowly turned back to him. "I am not interested in power," she said. "Far from it, I came to save heathens. We all did. Look around. We are risking our lives to save your people."

What she said was true – the Westerners were helping his people from the wretched disease, but they were also bringing chaos. The kingdom was peaceful and harmonious before the foreigners came into their land.

"I've only just begun to gain the queen's confidence," she continued, "and I can't afford to lose it with trifles when a larger mission is at stake."

Once she had alluded to Henry about working the "head," and now, Han was beginning to understand her meaning of the "larger mission" – she meant to convert his people to Christianity by first converting the queen. Her agenda came first even if it meant breaking her oath. Han was seeing her truly for the first time, without the blind enchantment she had woven over him.

"Why should the head trust a person who has broken her promise to the body?" he asked.

Grace pulled the kerchief from her face. Up close she looked tired and she sighed. "What would you like me to do for you?"

"Please ask the queen to give audience to Master Yi's ward,

Ji-nah. She has proof that he has been kidnapped by the tutor. She must arrest the tutor and interrogate him for the master's whereabouts."

Grace's head was bowed and her eyes closed. When he had finished, she opened her eyes and looked at him incredulously, as if he had asked her to fetch him the moon.

"I'm no miracle worker. The request you make is beyond my talents."

"There's more," he said. "I think there's a larger conspiracy that the tutor is involved in led by a Japanese named Miura Goro."

"Miura Goro?" Grace perked up all of a sudden.

"You know him? This information came at a great cost. My mother – " His voice cracked but he continued. "She heard the tutor and Goro's minion conspiring about some order he was to give."

Grace's eyes flickered in recognition to something and she pulled her apron off. "I will go to court – and do my best to keep my promise," she said.

The dangerous name meant something to Grace. Whatever it meant, she was on her way to alert the queen, and perhaps she would pull off the miracle for him, after all.

CHAPTER 29

It had been days, but still no word from Miwon. While she wasn't expecting a royal invitation to whisk her away to the inner chamber for an audience with the queen, she did hope for something – some acknowledgement from the queen, at least. Was she foolish for divulging such an intimate secret as her birth mother's name? Amah said the name meant nothing to many in court because her ghostly pale, blue eyes made her a pariah even to her clansmen. But, even if her mother's abnormal eyes made her unlucky, she was still a Min and that made Ji-nah a kinsman. Wouldn't that give her some credibility with the queen?

Ji-nah searched for Miwon and hoped to get a response, but the girl ignored her searching gestures, leaving Ji-nah with doubts and regret over her own impulsive nature and misplaced trust. She scolded herself, but what alternative had she in the *nain* quarters? *Laundry and mounds of it,* she thought. Everyone seemed to have deserted her. Hee-sun, who eventually forgave her for not revealing her guarded secret, was too busy in the kitchen with the foreign visitors coming daily to the palace. Even the little ones, Hana and Duri, were busy being schooled by Westerners at the new girls' school the missionaries had built with the queen's sponsorship.

Something was happening, as if the storm charge in the air

had stirred things up. Had the court adapted Western ideas as her master had been suggesting? By Hee-sun's description of all the foreign dishes, it seemed that the hermit kingdom had become a worldly place. A school. Ji-nah wondered what would be taught by Westerners. The girls would not learn their *Hanja*, nor the disciplines of Confucius; it made Ji-nah wonder what girls in the West learned. Her tutor's often quoted axiom came to mind – *east is for the East, west is for the West*, but what did that mean anymore when their kingdom has opened its doors to the Westerners?

She remembered Master Yi telling her that no one culture is all powerful – even China, Korea's protectorate state that had for centuries been the epicenter of all culture and power, has been weakened. *We can always learn from those that are different from us,* he had said to her, *but never forget who we are.* Oh, how she wished he were here to help her sort through the changes that were happening in the kingdom. Such thoughts swirled in her mind as she continued her endless boiling, skimming and wringing.

The bright linens, fully dried now, fluttered on the line. Ji-nah was taking them down when Second Attendant surprised her with cold barley tea. The unusual kindness took Ji-nah aback, and she suspected a certain coaxing before a more arduous assignment.

Ji-nah accepted the tea with both hands and waited.

"There's been a steady stream of work for you," said Second Attendant. "The others say you've been doing your share."

Ji-nah bowed, still unsure of the meaning of this encounter.

"Go on, refresh yourself," said her taskmaster.

Ji-nah took a small cautious sip.

"You've proven yourself obedient and diligent with what you may have first called menial when you arrived. You're shedding some of that arrogance," said Second Attendant. "Therefore, I'm promoting you."

Hope stirred and she wondered if she might be promoted to the inner court. Might Hee-sun put in a good word for her? Before her hopes could run ahead and get her into trouble, she bit her lips and waited.

"Yes, it's true. You will not be assigned to laundering forever. Something more appropriate." She cleared her throat. "The queen would like to send one of her finest to help the foreigners. You'll be doing your part to help improve relations and help our kingdom."

Could this be true? The queen asked? Perhaps Miwon did put in a good word for her. "Might I thank the queen for this opportunity?" Ji-nah asked.

Second Attendant scowled, making Ji-nah think she was being presumptuous, but her thick dark eyebrows relaxed some and a sadder expression came over her face. "You'll be working at The Shelter, child."

"The cholera hospital?" Her high soaring hopes came crashing down like a kite cut from its string.

Second Attendant nodded. Her lips were smiling, but her eyes were full of pity. It was a death sentence to be sent where the rat disease ran rampant – they said that it's the foreign constitution that keeps them immune to the foul illness, but sending a Korean was a punishment. She thought of Miwon and what she might have told the queen to get her into this injurious predicament. Oh, how she wanted to tear the wig off that arrogant girl.

"But how was I chosen for this assignment?" she asked.

"I don't know, but you've been requested by name."

"By whom?" Ji-nah asked, knowing full well Miwon had betrayed her, but she still wanted to hear it. But Second Attendant only shook her head.

A death warrant had some benefits: no more laundering and a chance to ride the palace palanquin. The court wanted to make a grand gesture and it was arranged that Ji-nah be taken to The Shelter as a person of privilege than walk as *nain*. It was a small consolation, though Ji-nah would have preferred an audience with the queen.

She braced herself for a dark and gloomy place where she expected pestilence to lurk and death to wait for the dying, but the small brick compound that housed the patients was surprisingly bright and clean. The sick lay in an open room partitioned off by low folding screens. From a dozen or more occupied beds came low ailing moans and the occasional violent retching that filled the room. Busy hands carrying pails and rags were cleaning off discharge and vomit while a few nurses tended to the sick patients. Nobody noticed Ji-nah's arrival.

Eventually, one worker caught Ji-nah idling and scolded her for it. She shoved a large kettle into her hands and told her to collect water at the pump and boil it in the kitchen. The urgency in the room spurred her into motion without question. Surprisingly, she needed no further instructions and managed to do as she was asked. She wound her way around the back of the building and after filling the kettle she brought it to the cook in the kitchen where they were making briny broth to help relieve the dehydration the patients suffered.

The workers all wore a kerchief around their mouths but Ji-nah, having just arrived, had the distinction of a bare face. A tall woman in a dark blue frock was approaching as if to reprimand her. The woman's foreign attire was shockingly immodest, revealing her narrow feminine curves. It was a stark contrast to Korean ladies, who wore ballooning high-waist skirts that hid the feminine shape. The foreign woman's narrow, blue eyes reminded Ji-nah of her mother's unusual pale eyes. A cross dangled from her collar.

Realizing that Ji-nah was a newcomer, the lady removed her kerchief tied over her mouth. "You must be Ji-nah from the palace. Thank you for coming to help." She bowed politely. The foreign lady spoke her language, but her unusual pronunciation made Ji-nah listen with care.

"How do you know me?" Ji-nah asked. Miwon had mentioned a foreign lady making inquiries, but in all her excitement, Ji-nah had forgotten to ask the arrogant girl about that encounter.

"My name is Grace Abbott, and I am a friend of Han's."

Ji-nah was confused. "You know Han? But the queen sent me here."

"Yes. I called you out of *nain* duties as a favor to him."

Han, the manor's servant? What kind of influence did Han have over this foreign lady to gain a favor? Ji-nah was dumbfounded and certain she looked equally puzzled.

The lady gave a knowing smile and explained to Ji-nah as if she were slow. "Han is well, if you're wondering. He's at the mission working to help save your people from sin and disease." The foreigner possessed no refinement of a *yangban,* but spoke directly, if not arrogantly.

"Were you the one asking Kim Sanggung about me?"

Grace nodded. "Han asked me to inquire about you at the palace when he heard you were sold to the palace by your tutor. Han was concerned about you, and he explained everything about your family situation."

"Then you know that Master Yi is kidnapped," Ji-nah said.

The lady nodded. Ji-nah realized she might have an ally. "We need to alert the queen and have her make an arrest for the tutor. I'm sure he's behind some bigger conspiracy to harm the master and endanger the queen." The lady's sudden aloofness made her wonder who this woman really was. "How was it that you could have called me out of my *nain* duties?" Ji-nah asked.

A sly half-smile spread across the lady's face as if she was waiting for Ji-nah to finally ask. "I'm the queen's physician," she said.

The queen trusts a foreigner for her most intimate conditions? Ji-nah wondered what the master would think.

"Then you have her confidence." Ji-nah hoped she could avoid Kim Sanggung, who refused to believe her.

The Westerner nodded.

"Then you must help me. You must get me an audience with the queen, or at least tell her that she must arrest the tutor and interrogate him. Only then will she find Master Yi and uncover the tutor's treasonous plots –"

Grace's lips tightened and held up her hand like a Buddha. "Han's told me everything," she said. "But I am no miracle worker. Do you know that the queen has threats daily on her life? She has surrounded herself with Westerners, like myself, because she trusts no one – not even her countrymen, some who have sided with the Japanese to overthrow the royal family. I did my part in helping you, but I cannot risk the queen's confidence in me." She put her mask back on and headed back to work.

Something was amiss though. Why was this lady so vested in the queen? What was she after? In her utter frustration, Ji-nah shouted after her, "Saving Master Yi will save the queen!" But the lady had already turned the corner.

CHAPTER 30

Armed with their circulars, the boys had combed through the clustering neighborhoods and a few fringe shacks along the river. Making their final rounds, they headed toward the edge of the city walls when Han made an excuse to break off from the brothers. His feet seemed to have a mind of their own, leading him down the familiar, winding lane through the bamboo groves that took him back to the Yi Manor. It was only a few months since he had been away and the manor looked as it always did, with its imposing walls, but it felt different – less inviting, more menacing now that it was used as a traitor's lair.

Across the lane stood Master Cho's house, where Boram used to serve. The house was empty now, but someone had boarded up the gate and posted a sign on the pillar that read: DESERTER – KING'S PROPERTY. *Yangban* families had been leaving the capital in droves because of the growing riots. Japan's victory over China had created an air of uncertainty, and conspiracies and court intrigue abounded. Officials were being arrested on trump charges against the crown that many were fleeing, despite having their property seized and being labeled as cowards and traitors. It was a confusing time for the kingdom, making Han wonder what kind of mayhem the tutor was contributing behind the manor walls.

One of the boards on the Cho's gate hung loose. Han stuck his arm through a small opening and managed to wedge it open wide enough to slip into the Cho courtyard. On the other side of the wooden gate, a large knothole provided a clear view of the Yi Manor. He wasn't planning to make an outpost for himself, but he wondered why he hadn't thought about spying on the tutor before – perhaps he would find clues to where the master was being held.

He dragged a straw mat he found in their courtyard and nestled down by the gate like a watchman. Not long after he situated himself, there was some activity along the lane – a band of ruffians with white bands tied around their heads were led by cropped-haired men in dark Japanese robes. Could one of these Japanese men be Miura Goro? He couldn't forget the name of the leader who was supposedly going to "give the order" to something important and dangerous to the master and their kingdom. The Japanese men all wore the same kind of robes with no distinction in rank – Miura Goro could not have been one of them, but Han took care to note each face that entered the manor.

The men remained in the manor as the shadows grew longer. By now, the brothers were probably returning to the print shop, and though Han wanted to keep post, he knew he would have to return before it got too dark. As he was preparing to leave, something bumped against the other side of the gate. The thump repeated. Whatever made the noise, Han couldn't see it through the knothole. *Probably a stray animal*, Han thought as he pushed the hanging slat and squeezed through the boards out onto the lane.

With grizzled hair and tattered rags, it looked like an animal, but it was clearly human: a beggar wedged tightly between the pillar and the gate, his elbows bumping against the wood for support. And like a startled animal, the beggar sharply turned his head when Han emerged. They stared at one another, both frozen in fear, until the beggar rose from his hidden pose and started toward Han with a wild, crazy smile, exposing a set of blackened teeth. Scared out of his wits, Han ran.

Halfway down the lane, Han heard the Yi Manor gates rumble open. A string of malicious taunts ensued.

"What's this? Look, a crazy dog!"

"Let's have some fun with him. Ya!"

"He smells like the deuce!"

Han stopped, half-curious but also half-guilty for leaving a poor beggar behind with a gang of bullies. He watched helplessly as they pelted stones at the beggar until their rowdy jeers brought Tutor Lim out from the manor.

"Quiet, you fools," the tutor warned. "You'll bring trouble and compromise the plan."

Their boisterous laughter turned to low grumbles. They continued to kick up dust at the helpless beggar, curled up in a fetal position.

"Enough! Get him out of here," the tutor ordered, flicking his switch before the ruffians.

The men complained about the stench, but eventually two unlucky ones picked up either ends of the slumped figure as the tutor surveyed the lane. The tutor noticed Han's figure in the distance, but before he could be recognized, Han ran out of sight.

His heart was racing at the sight of the old villain; Han felt foolish for running, tucked-tail like a coward. Where was that thirst for vengeance when he had seen his battered mother? Though he knew he should head back to the mission, his legs carried him toward the teahouse. He would check on his mother.

When he got to the teahouse, it was deserted and even after several calls, no one answered.

"*Uhmunee*," he called for his mother again as he wandered down the corridor. He slid open the door to one of the bedrooms and instantly recognized the stale scent. He had been around The Shelter long enough to recognize the stench of the disease. Next to a rumpled bed were soiled linens, upturned bowls, and burnt moxa.

He raced out of the teahouse praying, *please be there, please be there*. If his mother had made her way to The Shelter, there was still hope. She would be all right.

He was still panting with shallow breaths as he stood at the doorway of the patients' floor. Finally he found the teahouse lady rocking nervously at the far end of the room. But something felt wrong.

Won-jin and John Abbott were hunched over a still figure, praying.

"Mother!" Han cried, pushing them aside. Her listless body lay stiff as a corpse, but she was still breathing. In just a short time since he'd seen her, the illness had taken its toll, ravaging her health, turning her full cheeks into old dried apples. A bluish, otherworldly hue spread over the fading bruises on her face.

"Mother," he cried again, shaking her. "How could this be?" He turned to John.

"Tainted melons," said Won-jin.

"Had she come earlier, we might have been able to help ..." John said.

His mother's eyes were fluttering beneath her closed eyelids. He shook her again and buried his face into her bosom. A low groan rose from deep within her chest and he looked up. Her dry, cracked lips barely parted.

"So tired," she whispered.

"Mother, I'm here," he said. "You'll be all right."

His mother's eyes struggled to open. When she found his face, she looked like her old self again, with laughter in her eyes. But her strength quickly faded and she whispered hoarsely, "Han, you're a man now."

Her words seemed more than a mere acknowledgement of his manhood, but a recognition of how she saw him. She, who kept her praises for her son hidden for fear of evil spirits taking notice, kept true to her nature and buried her heartfelt sentiment in plain words. He wiped the blur from his eyes and saw a faint smile appear on her lips. She was proud of him. And in that moment, he thought he saw something like relief come upon her countenance, and a tight knot formed in his stomach because he knew those were her last words.

The faint smile stayed, but her gaze, still fixed on him, was vacant.

"No! Don't go!" he cried, holding the hollow vestige of his mother. He wasn't ready for her to leave. How could she abandon him? He knew that she had let go because she felt he was ready, but he didn't feel that way. "I still need you," he whispered through his sobs.

"Is it too late?" someone said behind him. A bowl of broth dropped and a wet hand gripped Han's shoulder. "Han, *oppa*!" It was Ji-nah's quavering voice. *Oppa*. He was always Han, the servant – not older brother. He never expected to be addressed with such familiarity, such intimacy. But nothing about today was expected. The surprise of seeing Ji-nah was eclipsed by his heavy heart, and at that moment, Han had little thought of anything else. His mother was gone. Why couldn't he have done more for her? He had those useless circulars to teach everyone else about the illness, while here was his mother dying of the wretched disease that even The Shelter couldn't help.

Jejang.

Ji-nah was wailing over his mother's body; the sight of it made him furious.

The damn tutor. If it weren't for him, they would all be at the manor where no rat disease could touch them. He pulled Ji-nah away from the shell of his mother when something fell from the bedside.

A cat talisman.

The superstition had cost his mother her life. He had left the circular and even told her how to keep safe from the rat disease, but she was insistent on the old ways, even until the very end.

CHAPTER 31

All the tears in the world could not alleviate the smoldering pain of grief. The thought of Amah gone from this world forever left an unreal feeling, as if Ji-nah were caught in a bad dream she couldn't wake from. She could no longer bear working in The Shelter where the memory of her nursemaid laid stiff on the cot brought her a fresh stab of pain. Mercifully, Grace Abbot sent her back to the palace where she would return to her duties.

Second Attendant was understanding, giving her space to grieve, but with the frenetic atmosphere in the palace, Ji-nah felt more anxious than ever about her father. What if she were to lose him, too? Though she had no proof, there was a moth-like flutter of hope inside her that urged her to get to the queen. She didn't know what she would say, only that her father was kidnapped and that the queen too was in danger by the same hand, Tutor Lim.

Though he wasn't specific, her father's warnings about the queen's imminent danger seemed to be coming into fruition. All around the palace, there were signs: Japanese guards, Western visitors and threats of riots. She could no longer sit idle, waiting for Miwon or Grace Abbott. The arrogant girl seemed to have forgotten all about her request to mention the name of her mother, Min Yumi to the queen, and the Westerner – well, she never intended to help. Ji-nah had to do something. Time was running out.

Even her pendant seemed to agree, making itself weighty and felt. She clutched her hand around the warm jade as her mind whirled. She would pay dearly for approaching the queen without a proper summons, but she no longer cared about her own fate. Besides, once the queen found out she was a Min, Her Majesty was bound to pardon her. Wasn't she?

There weren't many ways to infiltrate the inner court. She contemplated disguising herself as Miwon, stealing her clothing and headdress, but the problem was, she didn't know what the arrogant girl *did* in the inner court. Without Miwon's cooperation, she would only fumble about, trying to find her way to the queen, and get caught in the process. She closed her eyes in deep meditation, rubbing the petal as if it were a rosary. A preposterous idea worked itself in her mind. It was so simple, she wondered why she never considered Hee-sun, her only friend in the palace, for help.

The fact was she would be placing Hee-sun in great danger for her cockamamie idea, but she took a chance. Surprisingly, it took little convincing for Hee-sun to readily agree.

The banquet was in two days, and their preparations began straightaway. Late that night when all were asleep, Ji-nah and Hee-sun stole out from their quarters and made their way toward the kitchen, avoiding the night patrol. Silently, they walked behind the kitchen where a field of waist-high brown clay pots stood like a garden of giant toadstools.

"In here," said Hee-sun, pointing out a little nook between two jars. "You can hide in here."

"Are you sure you want to do this?" Ji-nah asked. "You'll be punished if you get caught."

"I know what it's like to have a father; you don't," she said. "And you still have a chance to save him."

Ji-nah was dumbstruck. She couldn't say if she would do the same for her friend if it were the other way around. The sacrifice Hee-sun was willing to make overwhelmed her; she blinked away the blur in her eyes and squeezed her friend's hand.

Hee-sun explained the layout of the kitchen and who would be at which station. She also described in detail her own responsibility, the arrangement of the *surasang*, the more than twenty dishes that went on the royal table. Ji-nah took it all in and the two girls rehearsed one more night before the big day.

On the day of the banquet, Ji-nah feigned illness from her lunar cycle, an excuse that would normally not be acceptable, but Second Attendant was more lenient with Ji-nah ever since she returned from The Shelter. As Hee-sun had told her, Second Attendant really was all roar and no bite.

With the plan set in motion, Ji-nah went back to her room, pretending to take a rest. She unrolled her bedding and placed a blanket over some pillows, shaping it like a body, then snuck away toward the kitchen.

Crossing the vast courtyard in broad daylight posed an unexpected problem. The day guards were more alert than the sleepy night guards. She bit her lip and watched in vain as attendants passed through with hurried purpose. Hee-sun would be expecting her in no time. Then like a flash, she got an idea, rushing behind the laundry building where sheets fluttered on the line.

Carrying a damp bundle of sheets in her arms, she walked briskly across the courtyard under the guards' watchful eyes, but was undisturbed. When she reached the field of pots, she left the load of linens in one row and waded through the maze until she found the nook. Even in the daylight, it was a good hiding place.

Hee-sun arrived shortly, and the two girls quickly exchanged clothes.

"Here," said Hee-sun, handing her a bronze bowl. She removed the lid off one of the pots and scooped up some fermented radish into bowl. "This goes on the upper most right-hand corner of the table."

Hee-sun's detailed directions guided Ji-nah through all the steps from the kitchen to the reception hall where the banquet was taking place. Ji-nah wondered how long she could keep up the pretense before she was discovered, but more hands had been called to help with the banquet, and no one seemed to notice that Ji-nah was not supposed to be there.

Still she kept her head low, and made sure she was the last in the train of attendants that carried in the food. Because she carried the royal table setting, she was led down a separate corridor that led to the queen's dais. The entrance was flanked by two guards, and when she approached, one ordered her to wait.

"*Surasang* for Her Majesty," said Ji-nah.

"You know it has to be tasted," he said. "Leave it here."

"And I get blamed if it should be tampered?" Ji-nah said, surprising herself with her quick answer.

"Fine. Wait with it in the anteroom." He gave her an annoyed glance.

She set the tray down and waited, for what she wasn't sure. Hee-sun had said nothing about this. Finally, opposite the entrance, another set of sliding doors opened.

It was Miwon.

They stared at each other in silent amazement.

"What are you doing here?" they both said at the same time.

You have a purpose, Ji-nah reminded herself. "Hee-sun is sick, and they needed help for the banquet," she lied, but Miwon's piercing eyes seemed to see through her. "And you?" Ji-nah pressed, trying to deflect Miwon's doubts.

"I taste the queen's food," said Miwon.

"I thought you were hoping to be the prince's concubine –" Ji-nah didn't finish for Miwon's glare stopped her cold.

"Shows what little you know," Miwon snapped. "You and that nosy Hee-sun with your gossips. I serve to protect the queen." Miwon took a set of chopsticks from her sleeve and took a small taste from each of the bowls on the tray. When she finished, she called for an attendant, but Ji-nah gripped the tray.

"I can bring it to the queen," said Ji-nah.

"Nonsense," said Miwon. "That's not the protocol."

But Ji-nah's eyes were pleading.

"You're up to something," said Miwon.

"Please, Miwon …"

"You're lucky I'm not calling the guards."

"I must speak to the queen," she said. "I must get help to my master. I know he can help the queen."

"What you're asking would get us both into big trouble."

"You never asked about Min Yumi, but I have a right for an audience with the queen because I am her kin."

"You think I didn't ask?" Miwon said, incredulous. "The name Min Yumi meant nothing to the queen. She said, 'Never mention that dead name again.' I don't know what you're playing at, but you'll forfeit your life, and quite possibly mine!"

"Please, Miwon. I have no other choice," Ji-nah said, prostrating herself at Miwon's feet.

But Miwon seemed unmoved, her face set hard as stone, yet something flashed across her face when she caught a glimpse of the pendant that spilled from Ji-nah's bosom.

Ji-nah took it as a sign of approval and didn't hesitate to pick up herself and the tray. She made it out of the first set of doors outside the anteroom, but before she could get any further, Miwon grabbed her arm.

"I'll take you," Miwon said.

Ji-nah didn't understand Miwon's sudden change of heart, but if it was some trickery on the sly girl's part, it didn't matter. Maybe she wanted to see Ji-nah fail and lord it over her. Whatever her reason was, it was too late now.

Guests, foreign and noble, were seated in the brightly lit reception hall. The queen sat upon a dais behind an opaque silk partition. The chit-chatter of foreign tongues sounded like songbirds. Though Ji-nah wanted to take all this in, she kept her head bowed in reverence as she approached the queen's table.

"What is the meaning of this?" Kim Sanggung asked in a harsh whisper.

From the corner of her eyes, she saw Miwon bow before she spoke. "There is a matter that cannot wait. This *nain* has an urgent word for the queen."

"Your judgement is lacking, Miwon," said Kim Sanggung. "This is not the forum for such matters."

"It cannot wait," said Ji-nah, still stooped. Then turning to bow to the queen, she said, "Your Majesty, your servant Yi Yong-gi is in grave danger. He is kidnapped. He said you are in danger as well."

The chattering ceased and hushed murmurs filled the room as the guests seemed to be aware something was happening on the dais, behind the opaque screen.

"You're the impertinent girl from the Yi Manor!" said Kim Sanggung in quiet outrage.

"Take her out of here." She gestured to the standing attendants by the queen's side.

Hands on either side grabbed her. Panic shot through her and before she knew it, Ji-nah crumbled to her knees.

"Your Majesty, I am your kinsman!"

Silence fell upon the room. If there were to be a death sentence, surely the queen would not decree such punishment before distinguished guests.

"She's mad," said Kim Sanggung.

"Raise your head, child," said the queen.

Ji-nah obeyed, while trying to avert her eyes from looking directly at the queen. Still she could not deny herself a quick glance. The queen's beauty was simple, yet regal. She wasn't adorned in opulence, nor did she need it, for there was a definite air of authority emanating from her small frame. She was attractive with delicate features – almost too delicate with a swanlike neck that held up precariously a wig of braided coils upon her head. It was uncanny, the queen's resemblance to Miwon – down to the sharp falcon eyes, which the queen used to study Ji-nah, presently.

"Impossible," said the queen. "So impulsive, making such a commotion and in front of our guests, no less."

Miwon said the queen forbade the mention of Min Yumi, her mother who linked her to the Min clan. Was it her mother's ghost eyes that made her an outcast even to the queen? Still she had her father's letter. It would corroborate her story.

"My master, I mean my father, is Yi Yong-gi and he has been kidnapped. In his letter, he warned that your life was in danger, as well. Your Majesty, I beg you, please, arrest the tutor that resides in the Yi Manor. Interrogate him for he knows where my father is held. You should also know he is conspiring against you."

"Child, if I arrested every alleged conspirator, I would be alone in the kingdom," the queen said with some amusement.

Kim Sanggung added her chortles, which ceased the moment the queen's instructive gaze fell upon her. She nodded with understanding.

Ji-nah's short audience with the queen was over as the hands picked her up again. She could see through the opaque film that the party had quieted and all eyes were trying to decipher the scene behind the gauzy screen. Ji-nah took in the room, spotting Grace amongst the guests. Their eyes met for a moment, but Grace turned away, ignoring the plea in Ji-nah's searching eyes.

There was nothing she could do. Not a friend in the room to believe her. She thought of poor Hee-sun, the faithful friend who would no doubt be punished for her corroboration. Worse still, her father would be no more.

She was passed to Miwon, who would escort her out of the room, when suddenly the arrogant girl spoke up.

"You Majesty, she wears a pendant," Miwon said accusingly.

The queen's puzzled expression stopped the exit procession.

"Show her your pendant," Miwon whispered to Ji-nah.

Ji-nah was equally puzzled. What could the pendant do to incriminate her further? Whatever evil plan the arrogant girl had in mind, it at least bought Ji-nah time with the queen. She untied the hidden pendant from the inner bow of her *chima*. The pear blossom with a crooked stem was handed to Kim Sanggung, who brought it before the queen.

Naturally, the queen was unimpressed by the cheap trinket, but whatever transpired – the excitement of having a *nain* intrude upon her banquet – must have tired the queen, for she suddenly motioned to Kim Sanggung, and the lady-in-waiting announced Her Majesty's fatigue and urged all to continue with their festivities.

Though Ji-nah should have been more concerned about her own fate after ruining the queen's banquet, she was infuriated by the lady-in-waiting for not returning her pendant. The cheap bauble was her most valued possession, her only link to her mother.

Back in her room, anger swelled up to the tips of her ears, when Miwon's soothing words calmed her down.

"Her Majesty has summoned you."

CHAPTER 32

Han's life had changed forever, yet life seemed to carry on around him with no regard for the sudden loss of his mother. There was always work at the mission. People still needed to be fed, taught, or in the words of the brothers, loved and saved. But Han wanted to just stop all the activity around him and make sense of what had happened. One day he had a mother, battered but alive, and the next, she was gone. It was a strange feeling to think that he was all alone in this whole world with no family to call upon. It was a cheerless thought that made him feel exposed and scared. He wanted to hole up somewhere and be alone to think, but he was also afraid.

As if the old man knew his wish to be alone, Henry sent the brothers off to teach his people, while he kept Han in the print shop. At first Han was grateful for he couldn't bear the company of others, or helping them with their petty day-to-day needs. But the wooden blocks and the cold print apparatus proved to be poor companions and left him with his own miserable thoughts.

He hadn't realized how much he missed the brothers, especially Won-jin. There was something comforting about the boy's wordless presence that made him feel safe.

He laid out a block. ㅎ. A single consonant that meant nothing without a vowel. He spelled his own name: 한. The consonant now made sense with the other parts that gave it meaning.

At the manor, he at least knew who he was. His mother, Ji-nah and Master Yi were the other parts that defined him, giving him shape and a framework. He was a servant with hopes to become somebody, someday. That had given him security like an anchor. Now, he was alone and adrift – insignificant and meaningless like the single block.

In sheer frustration, he kicked the box of letters, sending the wooden pieces sailing across the shop floor. He'd have to pick up the scattered blocks, but the solid kick felt good for a moment. He swiped his nose along his sleeve.

"What happened?" said Henry, tip-toeing across the littered floor.

Han finished wiping the snot from his nose, and bowed deeply for his offense. What would he do, where would he go, if the old man threw him out?

Henry placed a heavy hand on Han's shoulder. The weight of his hand was steady, not condemning, but Han was too sheepish to look up.

"I'm sorry," said Han, his nose running again.

"It's I who should be sorry," said Henry. "You lost your mother, and I didn't even give you proper time to grieve. I'm sorry I can't offer you any comfort. Take some time, Han. Grieve properly."

Han said nothing. Was Henry dismissing him?

"No," said Han. "It was a mistake. I'll be no trouble. I'll clean up and work hard. I have to work …"

"My boy," said Henry. "Your work will wait for you."

Han shook his head, insistent. He had nowhere to go and if the mission didn't need him, he'd be begging out in the streets like the wild animal – like the man he saw the other day.

"Alright, then. Work if you must, but not out of fear. We will have a place for you here. We are family," Henry said.

Family? The missionaries had a strange idea of family – he and the round-eyes shared no resemblance – they didn't even eat the same kinds of food! Han's puzzled look must have begged for explanation.

"Indeed, in God's family, we are all brothers and sisters in the Lord. Why, we have the largest family in the world." Henry chuckled.

"But I am not Christian," said Han. "I do not have your faith."

"You may borrow mine for now," said Henry, patting him gently on the back.

Han began to pick up the scattered blocks. He felt better just for having Henry in the same room. He wasn't alone with his miserable thoughts. When he turned for the tray on the table, he realized that the old man was bent over, picking up the pieces along with him.

Before they had finished, the door flung open and the two brothers dragged in a filthy derelict who looked unconscious.

"We found this beggar," said Yong-jin, laying the beggar on the bench. "He was asking for you!"

"Has he got the disease?" asked Henry.

"No," said Yong-jin, "but he's been beaten, badly."

The smell off the man kept Han back, but the clotted wild hair and rags seemed familiar. It was the crazy beggar with the blackened teeth at the Yi Manor.

"We were traveling in your old neighborhood when we saw this figure slumped in a nearby ditch," said Yong-jin. "We thought he was dead, but he was making some gurgling noise. I didn't want to get close, but Won-jin reminded me of the Samaritan."

Henry's face broke into a knowing smile while Han was trying to understand Yong-jin's tale.

"The Samaritan is a story about a foreigner who was traveling and saw his enemy left for dead," said Won-jin slowly. "He helped him even when no one else would touch the dying man …"

"Later, finish the story later," Yong-jin said, waving his brother off. "It was strange. He kept saying 'Han' over and over. We thought he was talking about the River Han, and to take him there. Then he said he saw 'Han'. It's a common enough name, but we did find him near your old neighborhood. Do you know him?"

Han edged closer to the beggar whose eyes were fluttering in semi-consciousness. Even before Won-jin could nudge the man awake, a weight like an anvil dropped in his gut and took his breath away. The man opened his eyes slowly.

"Master!" cried Han.

"I knew it was you," said the man hoarsely. Even with blackened teeth and layers of grime, the broad smile that spread across his face uncovered the master Han remembered.

"We thought you were kidnapped! How did you escape?"

"Easy now," said Henry. "It might be too much for him."

One of the boys brought a cup of cool water. "I'm all right," said the master, wincing as he sat up to take a drink. "Just a bit dizzy." A wound on his head was visible even through his blood-soaked, matted hair.

"Those ruffians from the manor – they did this to you," said Han. A flush of shame rushed up his back as he remembered how he was no Samaritan.

"Yes, I was spying on the tutor," said the master. "But it looked as if you were, too."

Han nodded, unable to meet eyes with the man whom he had abandoned to the thugs. The master seemed to understand for he said, "I played the crazy beggar for a reason. They would never suspect me – and nor should you. They only hurt me, mildly."

By this time, the boys had brought Grace, who attended to the wounded patient immediately. Wordlessly, she cut his hair close to the scalp, washed the wound and dressed it. Han found it ironic that after all her resistance, or reluctance, to help the master, here Grace was saving him.

"This is my master," said Han.

Grace paused just enough to register what he meant. "I was told you were kidnapped."

"I was, but I escaped from Japan where I was held. Of all people, the tutor." The master stopped and for a moment Han thought he would burst into tears, but he laughed a mean and mirthless laugh before he turned serious.

"My captors are planning an attempt on the queen. She's in great danger, but so is my family with the tutor. I spent the last few days in the steerage of the *Hinomaru*, and went immediately to the manor to check on the family," he said. "That's when I saw you, Han. How is Ji-nah? And your mother?"

Han didn't know where to start. The present seemed to be the best place, for he couldn't bear to recount all the hardships before his mother's last breath. "She is no more," he said. The master closed his eyes and stayed silent for a long while. "But Ji-nah is alive, she is in the palace."

His eyes opened at the mention of Ji-nah, but they were full of sorrow. "It's all my fault," said the master.

"I have seen her," Grace said brightly, with an effort to

encourage. Then as if she remembered something, said no more.

"Does she know who she is?" the master asked Han.

Han nodded.

"It is a dangerous place for her then. Those who want Taewongun back in power want to destroy the queen and her clan."

"She serves as *nain*," said Han, trying to reassure him.

"Then for now, let her remain there where she is unknown," said the master. "It is a safe place for her."

Grace's face screwed up, as if she bit into a bitter turnip. "She may have revealed her identity."

"How do you know this?"

"I'm the queen's physician, and have privy to such information. Let me relay word to your daughter."

"She must stay hidden. A conspiracy against the queen is brewing," said the master. "You must tell her not to search for me – not until things settle."

"But your daughter will be most anxious for you."

"Once I am strong enough, I will call upon the palace. I will find her."

Grace frowned, but agreed.

The master was placed in Han's room for he needed looking after. Grace had given Han instructions to check on him during the night.

It was an odd but welcome feeling to care for the master in such an intimate way. That night, Han stayed by the master's bedside telling him all that had taken place at the manor. With closed eyes, the master listened. Soon soft rhythmic breaths ensued and Han pulled the covers over him. Han thought he had fallen asleep, but a trickle of tears ran along the side of his temple.

"You are brave, my boy," Master Yi said. "I owe you a mountain of debt that I can never repay." He opened his eyes and took Han's hand in his. "In my heart, I have treated you as my son because I have deprived you of your real father. He took the same poison as my wife that fateful day. I imagine he served the mistress faithfully until the end, accompanying her on the journey to the other side. And now, your mother paid with her life all because of this wretched curse on the Min name. If it were not for that, you would not be orphaned as you are now. But rest assured, Han, I am adopting you today as my own son. The manor will be yours one day."

Han was stunned. From the way his mother had forbidden the mention of his father, he had always assumed the man was some drunken lout with a sullied reputation. Now, the master was painting his father as a faithful hero. And he was adopting him as son. All this was too much for Han to fathom.

"But what of Ji-nah, your daughter?" Han said feebly.

"It was foolish of me to keep her from knowing her father, wasn't it. The lies we weave to protect the ones we love."

That night, Han went over all the secrets his mother and the master had kept from him and Ji-nah. They were all meant to protect them, yet what did it mean for them now? Sleep fell swiftly upon the master, but not for Han, who was an orphan that morning, but who found himself, by evening, with a father.

CHAPTER 33

What kind of influence did Miwon have over the queen that Ji-nah would receive a summons? As promised, Miwon brought Ji-nah to the queen's quarters.

By the time they had arrived, the queen had already taken off her heavy, ornate wig and changed into a simpler outfit. However, there was nothing relaxed in her manner. With eyes like daggers, she had the intensity of a cat ready to strike its prey by the time Ji-nah made her bow before her.

"Where did you get this?" the queen demanded, the pendant dangled from her hand like a pendulum.

"It was my mother's. Min Yumi," said Ji-nah, her head bowed.

There was a long silence in which the empty space on the floor between her and the queen seemed to stretch eternally. Ji-nah found the suspense insufferable. She had to know what the queen was thinking. What did the "ghost eyes" mean to the queen? Though she wanted to sneak a glance, she knew it was a foolish risk. The queen was not one to be betrayed by her own expression.

"And your father?" the queen said evenly.

"Yi Yong-gi is my father. I have no proof to offer other than my word, and until he is released from his kidnappers, my word cannot be validated," she said. She was tired of repeating the same story that no one believed, and now that she had finally reached the queen, she couldn't bear the rejection from her as well. Perhaps it was fatigue or resignation that made her want to get her pendant and just go home.

"Your Majesty, if I am to be punished for speaking the truth, please allow the return of my possession. It is but a trifle to Your Majesty, but the only treasure I have."

"Such impertin –" Kim Sanggung began to reprimand, but the queen's slight raise of hand silenced her.

"You're mistaken," said the queen to Ji-nah. "It is not a trifle. Do you know who Min Yumi was?"

Ji-nah nodded, "She was my mother …"

It was a trick question that the queen didn't expect Ji-nah to know. Instead she pulled a long cord from around her neck. At the end hung a pendant, just like Ji-nah's, but with a reverse crook in the stem. The two stems latched onto each other perfectly, making a paired set of blossoms.

"Your mother wasn't just any Min," said the queen. "She was my sister."

There was a collective gasp in the chamber, but the queen continued. "You don't need proof. The moment I saw you, I knew. You resemble her in every way, even your brazen impudence, but not the pale blue eyes."

Ji-nah didn't understand the queen's meaning. It was unclear from her flat tone if the queen loved or despised her sister. But the fact that she held onto the pendant gave Ji-nah some hope that all was not lost.

"Then you believe me that my mother is Min Yumi," said Ji-nah weakly.

"Of course, child," she said. "One look at you is like seeing my sister as she should have been without the cursed eyes. No, it is not you I doubt, but your father, who has betrayed me."

"He would never betray you. He was kidnapped, I swear. And the tutor is responsible," Ji-nah started, explaining everything that had happened since the runner came to the manor late in spring. She continued, "There's been activity at the manor, which my Amah gathered before she was found out. The tutor is conspiring with a Japanese gang, and their leader, Miura Goro. I think you are in danger as well."

For a moment, the queen was silent again. "Where is this Amah of yours?" she asked.

There was a swelling in her throat that forced Ji-nah to swallow hard. "Dead. The illness took her only a few days ago."

"Most unfortunate. The man she speaks of, Miura Goro, is no ruffian but the new Japanese Resident Minister. I have heard his name in caution from another source, but I placed little credence for she is a foreigner."

"Grace Abbott?" Ji-nah asked.

"You surprise me, child. How do you know this name?"

"Amah's son Han had asked her to mention me in court. She didn't, did she?"

Kim Sanggung cleared her throat at this point. "The foreign lady *did* ask for you. But we both thought it best not to disturb Her Majesty with rumors."

The icy gaze the queen cast on her lady-in-waiting was enough to make even Ji-nah feel the goosebumps. The lady-in-waiting turned toward Ji-nah and bowed, deeply and reverently as if in apology. Then Miwon, following suit, also turned and bowed.

Only then did Ji-nah realize what all this meant and who she was. She was not only a Min, but the queen's niece. She was royalty!

"Your father still betrayed me," said the queen, sounding peeved. Then she burst into laughter, as if she finally understood a riddle. "He must really love you to lie to his queen. He had the whole world believe you were dead! He had bested me."

CHAPTER 34

Dizzy spells kept the master bedridden; his frail condition from the harsh months of captivity slowed his recovery. But even in his compromised state, having the master made the uncertainty of their situation seem bearable, even hopeful. Ji-nah would soon be told that her father was alive and safe, and when the master was well enough, they would all be reunited. But to what place would they return? The tutor still kept the manor and the thought nagged at Han. He wanted to do something about the tutor, but for now, the master needed to rest and recover.

When the master woke from his late morning nap, Han ventured to ask about the situation. "The tutor will be arrested soon, won't he?"

A shadow cast across the master's face and a frown set in. Han couldn't tell if it was his injury or the reminder of the tutor that caused the master pain.

"The queen will do nothing," said the master. "Not for a long while."

"Why?"

"Because she has no power. The court is weak."

"But the king surely has power?"

"King Kojong never had any real power," said the master. "And now that the Japanese have moved into court, their officials are watching the royal's every move. They are forcing their will upon our government … We have no power."

"How can we allow such injustice? What can we do?" said Han, shocked by the weak state of the court – of his people. "Will you ever get your manor back?"

"The tutor is working with powerful people. Taewongun and the Japanese have forged some sort of alliance."

"But I thought the tutor hated the Japanese? He's a traditionalist who hates all foreigners," said Han.

"Sometimes, you have to work with one enemy to defeat another. If it were just King Kojong, the Japanese would have imposed their rights over the kingdom already, but the queen is their biggest obstacle. She and her supporters have been resistant of Japanese victory over Korea. That's why the Japanese tried to get rid of me. Get me out of court so I could not lend help to the queen. All the while I've been held captive, they've tried to indoctrinate me to see things their way."

"But that's not going to happen, right?" asked Han, unwilling to believe how desperately weak his country was, but he shouldn't have been surprised. The signs were all around him – the poor gathering daily for a scoop of rice from foreigners, the skinny brown-skinned kids collecting food along the dirty banks of the river, and the thousands upon thousands who didn't know their letters. Han felt helpless, but wanted desperately to do something.

While he couldn't affect change in the government or the Japanese, he could at least prevent the tutor from carrying out the conspiracy against the queen. There was something brewing in that manor and Han was going to find out.

"Master, are you feeling well enough?" he asked.

The master raised one thick eyebrow, but eventually nodded.

"I will resume my duties at the print house," Han said, lying to his master.

The master agreed that it was the least they could do to repay the foreigners for their kindness.

Han lied to Henry too, keeping the pretense that he was helping the master. But his real plan was to spy on the tutor. If he were to find out about the conspiracy with Miura Goro against the queen, then the high act of treason would forcibly put the tutor in jail.

For the next few days, Han would leave the mission in the predawn hours and return behind the Cho Manor's gates where he would stake out the manor until hours past curfew. For all his staking out, there was little or almost no activity at the former Yi Manor. Then one day, a runner came to the manor with seemingly urgent news before he left. Han thought about chasing the boy down, but the runner's business soon became evident as the gate remained wide open. He was heralding a visit.

A small cadre of Japanese men in cropped hair wearing Western uniforms marched down the lane preceding a carriage. The carriage stopped before the manor gates.

The tutor with his Korean entourage waited in a receiving line.

The carriage door creaked opened. A thickly mustached Japanese dressed in a handsomely decorated Western uniform looked furtively around before alighting. Ignoring the welcoming party, he rushed through the open gate that swiftly closed behind the party.

This was no ordinary man. Han was certain this was Miura Goro.

Whatever the plan was, it was happening soon.

Han raced back to the mission, ran up the stairs to his shared room where the master was convalescing. Surprisingly, the master was up, groomed and dressed, sitting at the desk writing a letter. With his beard trimmed and hair in a top-knot, the master looked more like himself.

"Master, I saw him!" said Han.

The master stopped mid-sentence and crumpled the paper.

"So, you were spying again," the master said in mock disappointment. "Tell me what you saw."

Han began to describe the man he thought was Miura Goro, or at least someone as important. "He had a small entourage with him and he traveled by carriage. He looked as if he didn't want to be seen."

"Of course," said the master. "He wouldn't want to implicate himself with Taewongun and his supporters."

"What does this mean?"

"I believe it means that they are setting things in motion."

There was a quiet knock on their door, and Grace's face peered in. "Time to check on you," she said, not realizing Han had returned. "You're back, Han. I heard there's been extra work in the print shop?" She seemed to be testing Han, but the jig was up, because the master knew what Han had been doing the past few days.

The master started furiously scribbling another letter. His seal stolen, he used his own fingerprint to authenticate his letter, dipping his thumb into a red paste before pressing it onto the page. He rolled up his finished letter and handed it to Grace.

"Please deliver this to the queen. She must evacuate the palace. And you must make sure my daughter flees as well."

"I'm not sure she will listen," said Grace. "I've preempted this and suggested Her Majesty come and stay in the mission. But the queen has reservations as it is not a legation, and she fears the Japanese will force her back to the palace. They are watching her."

"Will your government safekeep her?" he asked.

Grace shook her head. "Despite our government's warning to not get involved in your politics, the missionaries are open to helping," she said with some consolation. "But our government is adamant and will not allow the legation to help."

"Only the legation holds sanctity for the Japanese," said Master Yi.

Grace shook her head slowly and her eyes that usually gleamed with cunning and strategy lost their spark. The enchantress who once worked miracles could offer nothing, and her fallen countenance filled Han with despair.

"Then we go to the Russian legations tomorrow!" declared the master with thunder in his voice.

That night, Han lay in bed tossing. The promise for a better future was in the hands of foreigners who could do nothing to help their kingdom. *Tomorrow we go to the Russians*, the master had said. How were the Russians any different than the Americans? He'd find out tomorrow. But tomorrow, he thought. Always tomorrow.

The unusually warm evening made him even more restless, and he gave up on sleep. Quietly he left his bed and dressed.

He didn't know what possessed him, but he found himself walking to the manor in the dead of night. Since there would be no sleep that night, he reasoned it would be best to keep an eye on the tutor.

From the bamboo grove, he walked along the perimeter of the estate walls, making his way toward the front gate. There was no need to hide inside the Cho Manor gates at this late hour; the pillars and shadow from the gate's roof provided ample coverage.

Not a minute seemed to pass before a dark figure worked the gate of the Yi Manor from the outside and managed to slip in, unannounced.

The man in black seemed to fit the description of the thief who came to the manor some months back. From a safe distance, Han followed the shadowy figure in through the gate left ajar. He trailed the man through the dark corridor to the single room that was still aglow with life. He heard the man murmur something into the crack of the door before he slid in. Han crept close enough to see two silhouettes talking.

"The deed is done," said the voice that did not belong to the tutor.

"Delightful! Simply delightful," replied the tutor gleefully.

The deed done? Han stumbled forward, accidentally smacking his cheek against the paper door.

"Who's there!" the tutor shouted.

Before Han knew it, the door flew open and the man in black had Han by the scruff of his jacket. He yanked Han into the room where he discarded him like a rag at the tutor's feet.

"You, miserable creature," said the tutor. "It was you, wasn't it, lurking around the other day, running away like a cowardly dog?"

Han lifted his gaze from the tutor's fine silk hem to the murder in his eyes. He wasn't afraid of the foul man who hid behind fine clothes, the very man who beat his mother and caused her death. Han tried to get up, but a foot pressed against his back, keeping him down on the ground. He tried turning, but the man's foot now traveled to the back of Han's head. Still, he caught a glimpse of the man's face. A purple birthmark – the man his mother identified as the runner.

"He asked you a question. It's not polite to ignore your tutor," mocked the man in black. The man took his foot off Han's head and gave him a swift kick in the gut. Han doubled in a fetal position. Before the man could kick him again, Han managed to get on to his knees and he looked up at his tutor. "What deed have you done?"

"Answering a question with a question?" said the runner, kicking him once more. Han fell back, knocking over the clock on the bookcase.

"Obviously, you're not a very good teacher, Lim-san," the runner mocked again. He was having fun, like a cat toying with its prey. He picked Han up by the scruff of his collar again, promising more violence, but the tutor interrupted.

"Enough."

"What did you say?" the runner dropped Han, and moved squarely in front of the tutor, challenging him.

"I said, enough," hissed the tutor.

"Now that it's done, Lim-san, you will do what the Japanese tell you to do." Like two stags with locked horns, the men stared at one another in a standoff. Only by the sound of breaking glass did they shake loose.

The runner was first to see what Han held in his hand.

Han's heart raced as if it would gallop right out of his chest, but he held steady with both hands the pistol he had managed to take from the bookcase. The power he felt in his hands gave him courage to stand up on his feet.

"Fool, that decorative piece isn't even loaded. Put that down," commanded the tutor, taking out his switch.

"What is the deed?" demanded Han.

The runner chortled, but the tutor answered. "Tomorrow our kingdom will have a new ruler, Taewongun."

Han's hand began to shake hard, but he kept the pistol on the runner.

"What have you done to the queen?"

"You're an ignorant boy," said the tutor. "You know nothing of the ways of the enlightened. The queen and her supporters were ruining our kingdom."

"But you side with the Japanese – to do what?" said Han. "You betrayed the master."

"He was the worst offender! As if welcoming western ways wasn't bad enough, he educates a girl, grooming her as if she were his heir. Goes against the natural order of all things sacred."

"That girl is his daughter," Han said, unable to contain his anger. It was foolish for him to reveal Ji-nah's identity to the tutor, but he wanted the traitor to know the truth. He wanted him to know that he hadn't won everything with his treachery. "You had a Min under your nose, and you didn't know it!"

In the silence that ensued, the tutor's face contorted, and his eyes flashed with violent sparks, but the pistol kept him in check.

"What do you plan to do with that?" asked the tutor.

It felt like an eternity holding steady the shaking pistol. One squeeze would end this foul creature's life, but Han deliberated.

"I thought so. The pistol is not for slaves," mocked the runner.

Pang!

Smoke rose from the end of the barrel, but the tutor was still standing. The surprised runner wiped the trickle of blood from the bullet nick off his cheek.

In shock, Han lowered the pistol and the runner charged at him, pinning him down and wrestling the gun free from Han's grip.

"I've run out of patience with this one." He cocked the pistol and aimed it at Han's head when something crashed through the sliding doors. The master charged into the runner like an ox. The two struggled for the pistol. A white robe whirled around the black of the runner. Han and the tutor cautiously circled around the moving blur, the herky-jerky motions keeping the bystanders at a distance.

The master pinned the runner down, but the man held firm the pistol. Before he could fire, Han stepped on the man's wrist, knocking the pistol loose. But the tutor picked up the weapon and held it firmly against Han's side.

At this, the master released the runner.

"I didn't think it would end this way," said the tutor. "I was hoping I could avoid violence – unbefitting of me."

"Is betrayal more fitting for you, tutor?" said the master. "There will be nothing but agony for traitors."

"On the contrary, it is you who is the traitor. Instead of adhering to the way of *yangban*, the Confucius ways that held this kingdom together for centuries, you foolishly feed that fox with foolish notions that has led her to turn her back on tradition. We should have finished you off when we could, but we gave you a chance to reform. That was our mistake, but it shall not be repeated." The tutor aimed the pistol securely on the master.

In the same instant, Han slammed into the willowy tutor. The pistol fired as the tutor fell to his side. The rogue bullet hit his accomplice. The runner felt for his chest and brought his blood-soaked hands up to his widening eyes before he crumpled.

The master reached for the tutor, but the wily tutor wriggled free and slashed his switch before the master. The master dodged the switch, and tackled the sinewy opponent, who put up a strong fight against the master's compromised strength. They banged against bookcases and cabinets, sending parchment and books all over the place. Their tussle toppled the oil lamp, and a single flame quickly caught onto the scattered papers.

The two continued their struggle as the flames spread.

"Fire!" Han shouted.

Both stopped fighting and turned their attention toward extinguishing the fire. With thick cushions, they beat out the flames, trying to contain the spread.

"Get water, Han!" shouted the master. "Waken the servants!"

Han moved quickly shouting for help as he made his way to the well. With sloshing pails of water, he returned to find Master Yi tamping down the flames, but the tutor was slowly creeping behind the master. He pulled out something out of his sleeve, and Han half expected to see the familiar switch, but it was the pistol.

Into the mayhem, Han threw one of the wooden pails, nailing the tutor in the head. The tutor lost his footing, and fell close enough to a flame that caught on the edge of his loose robe. Yet unaware, the relentless tutor got up once more to curl his fingers around the pistol. The flames quickly consumed the silk robe, and by the time he realized the danger, it was too late.

Screaming in terror, the tutor ran like a torch into the dark night.

CHAPTER 35

In the ensuing days, there were big changes for the *nains*. Ji-nah and Miwon were both moved into the inner court. Ji-nah no longer minded Miwon, but admired the arrogant girl greatly, not only for her sake, but for the queen. Tasting the queen's food was not a luxury as one might expect – Ji-nah knew all too well that poisoning was a real threat in court intrigue.

Hee-sun, however, did not fare well initially when the Kitchen Attendant discovered the girls' deception. Despite everything ending well, her superior scolded Hee-sun and punished her severely, kicking Hee-sun out of the royal kitchen. Ji-nah pleaded with the Kitchen Attendant on behalf of her friend, and surprisingly, Hee-sun's position was restored.

Ji-nah wasn't used to having people yield to her wishes. It was a new sensation that came with her new identity. Still she didn't want to get used to it for she knew how fortunes could reverse, and she did not want to tempt fate. If she learned anything in the last few months, it was that one does not boast in times of good fortune, nor do they despair in times of misfortune. She was still learning what it meant to have a queen for an aunt, and she did not want to abuse her privilege.

However, the matter of her father still lingered and she could not understand why the queen did not immediately dispatch guards to seize Tutor Lim for interrogation. The tutor knew where her father was held hostage. But she could not pester the queen further – it was in Her Majesty's hands, and Ji-nah had to trust her.

When the two were alone, Ji-nah felt her impatience rise. Though she bit her lip to keep from saying anything more, the queen must have sensed worry from Ji-nah's screwed expression.

"Why so downcast?"

Ji-nah said nothing, afraid her persistence on the matter might appear as ingratitude. But the queen was perceptive.

"Your father is one of my most trusted advisors," she said, reading Ji-nah's thoughts. Her small round lips spread wide into a broad and easy smile.

"He was the only man deserving of my dear sister," she continued. "While others shunned Yumi for her unnatural eyes, he saw beyond their prejudice and ignorant superstition."

"But I thought you despised her eyes, too. Isn't that why she was turned away from court?" Ji-nah asked, confused by the history of her mysterious mother.

An awkward silence only confirmed that she had offended the queen. Why was she so impulsive?

The queen cleared her throat. "We were orphaned. My sister and I only had each other. But I was to marry the king. What could I do? Those narrow-minded in court would never understand.

"Some sacrifices had to be made. But it wasn't as bad as you think. Your father marrying my sharp-witted sister was the best consolation. I wanted to spare her from malicious talk and gossip. They readily agreed to keep a distance from court, but they were always important to me.

"It was because of them that I survived Taewongun's wicked attempts on my life. More than a decade ago when he plotted a riot to overthrow me, I escaped in disguise to your parent's home. Even though the old hound was chasing me down, it was still the most splendid time I had with you and your parents – yes, she was carrying you, so you were there …"

Ji-nah listened with great care, soaking in every word, every nuance she learned about her mother. All these years, she had assumed her mother was nothing more than a poor beggar with no other choice but to give up her child. She had no idea her mother was one with such cunning and wit.

"It was all her idea," the queen continued, "that I shun her so that the court would find me isolated and vulnerable. Making me look weak would only added to my influence. Oh, the games we play for power …"

"If you have such fondness for my father, then why haven't you acted? Why will you not arrest the tutor?" she asked, regretting her words almost immediately.

"I see you have your mother's impatience!" the queen said sharply.

The reprimand might have continued, but Kim Sanggung, who waited in the anteroom with Miwon, announced a visitor. A moment later, Grace Abbott was ushered in.

"Your Majesty," Grace said. She took a deep bow before the queen and made a small curtsey to Ji-nah. Grace didn't seem a bit surprised to find Ji-nah in the queen's presence. "I bring you both news. If I may, Mrs Sill from the American legation has taken ill, and has asked me to come in her stead. The ambassador is doing all he can, but our government can make no promises for protection. She sends her regrets … however, the mission still makes an offer.

In fact, here is a letter I bring from the mission." She handed a letter to the queen while her eyes were fixed on Ji-nah.

The queen handed the letter to Ji-nah. "You have your heart's desire, child." Then turning to Grace, she said, "I thank you for the kind offer. Tell Lord Yi that I take his council seriously, but I will stand my ground here, in the palace. My protection will come legitimately by a recognized government, or not at all."

Ji-nah quickly read the letter. It was her father's hand – he was alive! But he wanted her to flee from the palace with the queen. Before Ji-nah could make any sense of all this, Grace started again, insisting that the queen take refuge at the mission.

"The situation is getting serious," Grace said. "There's been confirmation that a coup might be imminent."

"Please relay my wishes for a speedy recovery for the ambassador's wife," said the queen. Her mind was made up, and she was finished with this meeting.

Grace nodded as if she understood, yet she broached the queen once more.

"What do I tell Lord Yi about his daughter?"

"So, he acknowledges his daughter to me after all these years," mused the queen. She turned to Ji-nah, letting her know the decision was up to her.

After all these months of thinking she was an orphan, she was pulled by the demands of her father and aunt! She was torn.

"How is my father?" Ji-nah asked.

"He is safe," said Grace.

That was all Ji-nah needed to hear to make her decision. She hoped her father would understand – he was safe, but for now, the queen was not.

"If it pleases Your Majesty, I wish to stay in your service," said

Ji-nah. "But, might I ask leave to call upon him tomorrow?"

The queen closed her eyes and nodded in assent.

Ji-nah wasn't sure if it was standard protocol, but the attendants seemed unusually busy with evening preparations. Miwon, the food taster, was relieved of her dinner assignment, and disappeared for the rest of the evening. Ji-nah was given a room in one of the inner chambers. Where the queen slept was a mystery, for she rotated her bedroom as a precaution.

Even with all the power and authority the queen had, it seemed as if she were a prisoner in her own palace. Outside her compound, Japanese sentries had been placed alongside the royal guards. Ji-nah was told that they were placed to give added security, but it seemed as if the foreign guards were no more than spies, restricting the queen's movements.

It had been a long day. Her body, tired from so many months of worry, finally relaxed, and as soon as the bed was unrolled, she fell fast asleep. Sometime in the middle of the night, a pang in her stomach woke her. All the prior talk of poisoning had her wondering, but the truth was she had chosen sleep over supper. Now, she would have to wait until the kitchen reopened in the morning, but it was nearly impossible to go back to sleep on a stomach that grumbled and complained. She groped for her pendant, but realized the queen still kept it.

With an empty stomach and absent pendant, she was restless. She stared up at the ceiling. With her eyes now fully adjusted to the darkened room, she could make out the swirly cloud patterns on the colorful wooden beams. It still felt like a dream to have an aunt who was the queen. And tomorrow she would see her father.

Between her grumbling stomach and her active thoughts, sleep was impossible.

She threw off the covers, put on her robe, and slipped out of the room. It took a moment to get her bearings. The powerful moon illuminated the unfamiliar hallways that led to an open verandah. A flask of water left on the tray seemed to be waiting just for her. A good, long drink satiated her hunger, a bit. In the cool night air, she wondering how much longer before the sun came up. It wouldn't be too long, and the open air felt so much better than her stuffy room. She decided to wait until dawn, but before she knew it her head drooped and she was lying on the cool wooden floor. Her eyes popped open when the floorboards vibrated beneath her cheek. Wiping the drool from her chin, she woke in time to catch a dark blur of swiftly moving feet. The feet belonged to men: men who did not see her lying there in the dark, men who wore all black, men who ran down the corridor toward the inner bed chambers.

Panic shot through her, and without thinking of her own safety, she got up to follow the dark mass down the corridor, but sudden screams stopped her short. Doors slammed and men shouted.

"Where is she?"

"Where's the fox?"

"Give up the queen!"

"Slay them all!"

Grunts and groans, thumps and bumps, screams and wails flowed out of the dark corridor, like the gates of hell had opened. She froze, unable to move as long as the hellish sounds continued. She couldn't say for how long, but it seemed to go on forever. When the screams and shouts seemed to recede, she took a breath, moving closer toward the corridor. Then someone hollered behind her, "Stay back!" and a few of the palace guards rushed past her, down into the darkness.

She felt her legs again, and cautiously, she edged into the abyss. An electric light from one of the bedrooms cast an eerie glow that spilled into the far end of the hallway. Drawn like a moth to light, she made her way to the source. The garish light revealed much more than she cared to see. The nightmarish sight could not be unseen.

She stood in horror, paralyzed and dizzy as if she were planted ankle deep in the sandy shore while the tides pulled back. All the bedroom doors were torn off completely or hanging precariously on its broken hinge.

And there was blood everywhere. Floors were slick with pools of it, walls and doors were splattered with it, and bed mats and blankets were soaking in it. The bodies of slain attendants littered the rooms.

The door to her empty room was smashed in, but it was the only room spared of blood. She walked through the now empty wing of the compound, following a trail of dark, wet footprints leading out toward the back entrance.

She searched for her queen. She found a slumped figure wearing a silk robe embroidered with a phoenix, the queen's crest. It was Her Majesty's robe, but it was not the queen. It was Miwon.

She bit her lip, tasting her own blood with the salty tang that ran down her cheeks. Oh, brave Miwon disguised as the queen offered herself as a sacrifice!

But where was the real queen?

She walked in a daze, checking each bedroom. At the entrance guarding the lowliest room, lay the *sanggung's* fallen body. The room was empty, but for the white jade pendant.

Ji-nah picked up the pendant before following after the trail of blood. She did not think about what she would do once she reached the savage men, only that she needed to find the queen. By now the menacing shouts and malicious laughter of the thugs were replaced by the urgent directives of the palace guards as they swarmed the grounds looking for the queen in the predawn hours. Warm winds carried a hint of kerosene. A solitary guard shouted, "Over here! In the garden!"

She followed behind a couple of royal guards into the entrance of the garden where more than a dozen Japanese men dressed in all black – like the thief she had seen at manor not so long ago – huddled around something crackling and glowing. Their black masks revealed only the gleam in their eyes drunken with violence, like wild beasts reveling at their slain prey.

The handful of royal guards were no match for the brazen assassins still holding their drenched swords. When one of the Japanese assassins saw them across the way, he made a move to attack, but his leader held him back, as if to say there was no threat.

The two sides were motionless as the flames spread between them. Ji-nah wasn't sure what was causing the impasse, but she saw one of the royal guard in front of her shaking uncontrollably, weeping. A sickening wave of horror came over her, and suddenly she understood. The fire that they were all watching was the one engulfing the queen.

Her body mutilated and burned. It was unimaginable what the Japanese were doing to their queen – who could be so cruel, so vicious? The body was fully engulfed now, and one by one, the men in black retreated toward the back wall of the garden and disappeared into the night. More guards came through the garden, and orders to put the flames out rang in the air. But it was too late.

The dirty deed was done. Their queen was lost.

The guards she hid behind moved quickly to salvage the remains of the queen. She had a clear view of the most heinous image: the queen's charred remains. That wasn't her queen, nor was it her aunt. It wasn't even human. The remains were nothing more than a blackened … thing, and it made her sick that anyone could do this to another human being.

In one night, she had seen enough violence and sorrow to last a hundred lifetimes. That the brutes could kill their queen in such an ignoble manner made her blind with rage. She turned and ran.

Thoughts raced as quickly as her feet, as quickly as her tears. Why didn't the queen leave the palace and take refuge as Grace had offered? Why didn't she flee? Deep inside, Ji-nah knew the answer. The queen had refused to run; she would not cower in fear, but face her adversaries in her rightful place. There was no compromise. Still, the queen's bravery came at a costly sacrifice and Ji-nah felt as if something precious had been snatched away, unfairly. She still had the pendant, but the familiar object lost its comfort.

She kept running, leaving the palace grounds. There was nothing here for her now. She found herself running through the dark and into the unknown streets of Seoul. Dogs barked and roosters crowed from behind gates and walls, and still she ran, until she saw above the roofline, a faint cross in the horizon.

CHAPTER 36

REUNION

Hungry flames that licked the wooden beams and pillars in the study wing were soon tamed by the servants and neighbors who joined them, pouring pails of water and sand. When the fire was under control, Han and the master quickly set forth for the palace. They hoped they were not too late to reach Ji-nah and the queen for the horrible "deed" had been accomplished.

On the lane off against the side of the manor walls, a stray dog nosed beneath a draped body. By the uncharred bit of hem that peeked beneath the white sheet, Han recognized his enemy. Someone had mercifully moved the dead tutor's body.

The two travelers had no concern for the dead, but were on a mission to save those in the palace. In their sooty, battered state, they tore through the streets and crossed the river passing the mission.

For Ji-nah, the winding streets were deceptive, and the cross illusive. Lost in the city she had lived all her life, she slowed to a walk, backtracking to where she first saw the cross in the horizon. The morning mist was thick. At the end of the small lane, she looked down at two figures racing toward her. With nowhere to hide and nowhere to go, she did the only sensible thing – run back the other way.

One of the men was now jogging toward her. She kept running, but she couldn't outrun him much longer. Soon a hand grabbed her shoulder.

"Ji-nah!" said a familiar voice.

It was Han and her father not much further behind him. Overwrought with relief and joy, she collapsed into her father's embrace. Her head remained buried into his chest until his sooty jacket became drenched.

"Let me see you," her father said.

When she finally let go, they examined each other, as if they had returned from the dead.

"We must get to the palace," said Han.

"The queen is dead," said Ji-nah flatly.

"Are you certain, my daughter? The queen has escaped from such attempts on her life before," said Master Yi.

Ji-nah shook her head as fresh tears pooled and fell from her eyes. "All her attendants were slain," she said. "Oh, it was horrible! They've murdered Miwon. And the queen – they burned her body in the garden …" She sobbed all over again.

Ji-nah's account seemed to sink in and her father became aware that the queen was indeed gone. A wave of indignant anger washed over him, and he shook violently, weeping bitterly and helplessly.

Han and Ji-nah each put the master – no, their father's arm gently over their shoulders and the three trudged toward the mission.

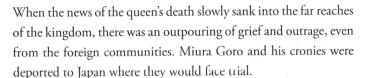

When the news of the queen's death slowly sank into the far reaches of the kingdom, there was an outpouring of grief and outrage, even from the foreign communities. Miura Goro and his cronies were deported to Japan where they would face trial.

Chaos in the government ensued. King Kojong, fearing for his life, found protection with the Russians at their legation. Their kingdom suffered greatly; even with Taewongun propped to rule, uncertainty loomed like a storm cloud promising to inflict more suffering.

The hermit kingdom could never return to the old way of things – the flood gates to foreigners and modernity had been opened, and like seawater mixing with fresh, it was impossible to separate the old ways from new. These were the last days of *eum-yang*, the last days of *yangban*, and the last days of the Morning Calm as they knew it.

Despite the inevitable closing of one chapter, Ji-nah and her father were hopeful of the kingdom's future. They would do what they could to help their country and their own lives. Master Yi's sustained injury required his daughter's assistance in his official capacity – though it was suspected that it was his ploy to spend time with his daughter, making up for lost time. They worked side-by-side mending and rebuilding confidence of the kingdom's leaders and foreign delegates.

The manor's reconstruction fell upon Han, the heir to the estate. He hired local boys from the streets, feeding and employing them. Remembering how he once envied Ji-nah for her prospect as *yangban*, he couldn't believe his childishness. The promise of the manor and the title of *yangban* were his now, along with the responsibility of taking care of Ji-nah. Though grateful, a strange emptiness stared back at him when he looked down the narrow tunnel of his planned future.

One afternoon, while the master and Ji-nah were on one of their many visits to the Russian legation, the brothers and Henry came to call on the manor. It was Han they had come to see.

"We've come to say our farewells," said Yong-jin.

"Where to this time?" The boys had been traveling to outer provinces with the message of their gospel.

"America. Back home for me," said Henry wearily. "I'm getting too old and tired for this young man's work. It's been good to work alongside you, brother Han. I wouldn't dream of leaving without saying good-bye." The old man stuck his hand out for a shake.

Han shook it reluctantly.

"We are going with him," said Yong-jin with vigor. "The church is sponsoring us. They'll train us properly for ministry."

Han's mouth hung open in shock, bereft of words. He had grown fond of these Christian friends, more than he cared to admit. The visitors left him with a hollow heart.

"The study is coming along nicely," said Ji-nah later in the evening.

"Hmm?"

"I said, the study is coming along nicely," repeated Ji-nah. "Are you listening?"

"Sorry. My mind was elsewhere."

"I can tell. What are you thinking about?"

"Oh, my friends are leaving Korea."

"The Christians?"

He nodded.

"They'll return, I'm sure."

"Not Henry," he said. "I'll never see Henry again, and who knows when the brothers will return."

Ji-nah was silent for a while. She knew that longing in Han's face. She remembered seeing it years ago when they would play by the boulder. "Han, *oppa,* you must go with them."

He shook his head and scowled as if she were suggesting something insane.

"I have always known your heart," she said. "Captain Han exploring the unchartered waters."

"That was a childish game," he said, surprised she would even remember the olden days. "I'm responsible for the manor – and for you. I cannot let your father down."

"You know him. He would want you to go abroad," she said. "And I can take care of myself."

"That's nonsense, you're a woman."

"We can't take care of ourselves?" she asked.

"All right, all right. But you know that's not what I meant. A *yangban* woman is kept inside, protected by male relations …"

"A new day is dawning, Han. The olden days of the Morning Calm will be a thing of the past. I will be my own agent. I have royal blood." She gave him a sly grin. "Besides, if we are to learn from Westerners, Grace has shown me what the future holds for women."

He shook his head in joyful disbelief. Where had that scaredy-cat little girl gone?

Two days later, Han was on a steamship headed for America. The master had provided for his passage in exchange for a promise that he would bring back a pistol to replace his collection. With all the warm good-byes, Han felt he was finally where he was supposed to be.

Henry took his rest in the cabin below, but the young men who had never been on a steamship stayed up on the main deck to watch their homeland disappear between the sky and sea. The brothers headed down to the cabins to warm up, but despite the cold salty wind and the rough waves threatening to knock him off balance, Han held fast to the ship's railing and made his way to the bow. Standing tall, he lifted his head and cast his vision to the horizon.

Acknowledgments

I didn't write this book alone. Of course, there were the endless hours of solitary writing, but the walks and coffees, workshops and discussions, and even extra schooling to improve my craft, were all part of the process that could not have been done without the love, patience, and encouragement of mentors, friends and family over the past ten years – that's right ten. It's been a long, but joyful, learning experience, and I owe thanks to God for divine appointments with wonderful people. Ten years is a long time, so my memory will probably fail when I try to recognize everyone who was so helpful and encouraging over the years, so advanced apologies for any lapse. My heartfelt thanks to Anita Teo, She-reen Wong and Mindy Pang at Marshall Cavendish International Asia, Scholastic Asia, and to the kind and dedicated people at SCBWI Singapore. Mentors, instructors, and friends: Stephen Roxburgh, Cynthia Leitich-Smith, An Na, Will Alexander, Shelley Tanaka, Meg Wivott, Beth Bacon, Jacqui Lipton, Steve Baker, Athena Hernandez, Kristin Routh, Lenore Appelhans Eisenhour, Naomi Laurent, Kekla Magoon, Tim Wynne-Jones, Kristie Choe, Pauline Wong, Nicole Heath, workshop groups and fellow writers and VCFA. Mom and dad: thank you for risking safety for an unknown life as immigrants – your journey makes me want to study my past. I'm most grateful to these incredible book lovers: Hannah, Hope, and DA – my earliest fans who inspired me and who would never let me give up – you guys are the future! And last but not least, to David, my biggest believer, my truest love, and my bestest friend.

Tina Jimin Walton is a Korean-American writer based in Singapore. She received her Master of Fine Arts in Writing from Vermont College of Fine Arts in 2016. A life-long learner who writes children's and young adult fiction, she teaches English and writing to teens.

Last Days of the Morning Calm is her first novel and was short-listed for the 2018 Scholastic Asian Book Award.